P9-BZP-872

Johnston, Velda
The Face in the shadows

THE
FACE IN THE
SHADOWS

Also by Velda Johnston

THE PEOPLE ON THE HILL

THE LIGHT IN THE SWAMP

THE PHANTOM COTTAGE

I CAME TO A CASTLE

A HOWLING IN THE WOODS

HOUSE ABOVE HOLLYWOOD

ALONG A DARK PATH

THE
FACE IN THE
SHADOWS

Velda Johnston

a red badge novel of suspense

DODD, MEAD & COMPANY

NEW YORK

ISBN 0-396-06303-9
Library of Congress Catalog Card Number: 78-156863

Printed in the United States of America
by Vail-Ballou Press, Inc., Binghamton, N. Y.

For Ann Stanwell, painter-actress,
to whom I owe the basic idea for this novel

one

Afterward it seemed ironic to Ellen that she had found the drugged child, not wandering in Central Park or asleep in some East Village doorway, but huddled on the terrace of the Cloisters Museum, that oasis of medieval tranquillity transplanted stone by ancient stone thirty-odd years ago from Europe to the upper reaches of Manhattan Island.

It was bright and cold and windy that May afternoon, the sort of afternoon when New Yorkers decide not to put their winter clothing in storage just yet. As she stepped from the Cloisters' shadowy interior onto the terrace, the cold sunlight was so blinding that she bumped shoulders with a stocky man going back into the museum. She answered his muttered apology with one of her own, and then moved across the terrace to the balustrade, a tall, gray-eyed young woman with dark blond hair and a high-cheekboned face that would have been classic except for a too-wide mouth.

Turning the collar of her plaid wool coat up around her ears, she looked at the New Jersey shore, now hazed with spring green, and then down at the wind-ruffled Hudson. Today it was so brilliantly blue that one could almost forget about the foul murkiness beneath that white-capped

1

surface, and imagine the river unchanged from the time when the *Half Moon*'s crew had sailed up it, marveling at its clarity, and at the fish teeming alongside the vessel, and at the "faire, spicey odours" drifting to them from the lush green banks.

She glanced at her watch. Almost two. Time to go home, she decided reluctantly, and call her answering service. Perhaps her agent had left some word about that coffee commercial. Perhaps, too, Charles had tried to reach her, to tell her that he had changed his mind about calling off his divorce. . . .

She turned back toward the museum's entrance. It was then that she saw the child, huddled in one corner of the terrace, and screened by a tubbed evergreen from the view of anyone moving only a yard or so out from the doorway. She sat on the flagstones, eyes closed, with her cheek pressed against the wall, and her hands lying loosely, palms upward, in the lap of her pleated maroon skirt.

Hurrying across the terrace, Ellen crouched down beside the small figure and touched her shoulder. "What's the matter? Are you ill?"

She didn't stir. Ellen grasped the thin shoulder, which felt kitten-fragile in her hand, and gave it a gentle shake. "Wake up! Answer me!"

The curly dark head turned. Big gray eyes opened. For a puzzled moment Ellen couldn't think of whom the child reminded her. Then, with a stir of an old anguish, she knew.

The pupils of those wide-set gray eyes, Ellen saw now, were contracted to pinpoints. The child muttered, "Leave me alone," before she closed her eyes and let her cheek sink back against the wall. Motionless with shock, Ellen stared at the white face, It couldn't be. Oh, you knew such things happened. Children this young, or even younger, took drugs. But it was hard to believe it of this girl, with her fine-featured face and her maroon school uniform with the monogram "M.S."—no doubt for Mainwaring School—on its jacket pocket.

Ellen glanced around. Still no one else on the cold, windy terrace. Again she shook the thin shoulder. "You've taken something, haven't you?"

The curly dark head rolled until its back rested against the stone wall. The long-lashed eyelids twitched, then opened. It seemed to Ellen that the child stared at her from far away, from some gray world where she wandered alone, unreachable. Had she sniffed the stuff, Ellen wondered, or were there needle marks on the arms hidden by the maroon sleeves?

Ellen cried, "Where did you buy it?"

The pale lips stirred. "Don't—buy. They give it to me." Again she rested her cheek against the wall and closed her eyes.

Ellen stared down at her, wondering what to do. Were the child's parents somewhere inside the museum? Almost certainly not. Mentally she reviewed the visitors she had noticed during her half hour of wandering through the Cloisters. On this chill Monday, there had been only a few. A cheerful, chattering group of about ten elderly men and women, perhaps members of some senior citizens club, who had been leaving the museum just as she entered it. A twentyish couple, probably honeymooners, who had stood hand in hand before the fifteenth-century tapestry, "The Hunt of the Unicorn." Three Japanese men aiming cameras at a courtyard fountain. A college-aged girl who had sat sketching the statues of the Three Kings. And, seated in the

3

chapel's Romanesque dimness, an elderly woman, wearing dark glasses and a man's woolen scarf tied over her head, who had looked like the sort of derelict you see searching through litter baskets on Second Avenue. Surely the child didn't belong to any of them. As for the man with whom she had collided in the doorway, probably he hadn't even seen the small huddled figure, not unless he had braved the cold wind to stand at the balustrade near the spot where she herself had stood.

Should she call a museum guard? Ellen shrank from the idea. It might mean the police, publicity. If she could find out the girl's name, where she lived . . .

The strap of the child's bag had slipped from her shoulder. The bag itself, a brown suede one ornamented with fringe, rested on the flagstones. After a moment, Ellen unclasped it. Its owner didn't stir. The first thing Ellen saw was a cheap white envelope, letter-sized, folded over once. Aware of an inward shrinking, she opened it. Three small packets of some sort of transparent plastic, two plumply filled, the third with part of its contents apparently gone. She closed the envelope, put it back in the bag, and took out a red leather billfold. It held three one dollar bills and two identification cards. One gave her name, Cecily Vandering, a Fifth Avenue address, and a phone number. The second, issued by the Mainwaring School, gave not only her name and address, but her birth date. She was older than Ellen had thought. In August she would be twelve.

Placing the first identification card in her coat pocket, Ellen restored the billfold to the fringed bag and then grasped the child's thin arm. "Cecily." The gray eyes opened. "Come on, Cecily. Come with me."

The child stared at her dazedly for a moment and then, evidently responding to the sound of her own name, got shakily to her feet. As Ellen led her through the doorway and into a corridor, its paving stones hollowed by the sandaled feet of monks centuries dead, she reflected with fleeting wryness that today she had hoped to refresh herself in the tranquil atmosphere of an age-long past, and thus gain strength to deal with her own far-from-tranquil present. One problem that faced her was Charles's defection, and her own attitude toward it. Was she sorry, or on the whole relieved, that Charles would probably go back to the almost-divorced wife from whom he had been separated for three years? Another problem was financial. Her residuals from a TV margarine commercial, which had held up nicely for almost a year, had dwindled to nothing this past month. And this summer, with her twenty-eighth birthday several months behind her, she might be considered a bit too long in the tooth to play the kooky teen-age bride in a straw-hat production of *Barefoot in the Park,* as she had for the past three summers.

But here, where she had hoped to immerse herself in the healing simplicity of an age-long past, she had found a child victim of the ugliest modern scourge.

Docile as a puppet, Cecily allowed herself to be led through the Cloisters' hushed dimness. As they neared the twelfth-century chapel, Ellen saw the old woman, the one with the dark glasses and the woolen muffler tied around her head, standing in the doorway. Sensing the curious gaze behind the glasses, Ellen quickened her pace, drawing the child along with her. They turned down a branching corridor, and then climbed stone stairs toward the parking lot and its outdoor phone booth.

5

They were only a few feet from the booth when a taxi drove into the parking lot. A middle-aged couple got out. Changing direction, Ellen led the child to the cab. "Will you wait a few minutes?"

The driver's gaze went from Ellen's face to the child's drowsy one and then back again. "Have to charge you."

"All right." She opened the door. "Get in, Cecily. Wait for me." Then, to the driver: "Will you see that she—?"

"I'll watch her." From his tone, pitying and yet wearily cynical, she knew he had recognized the significance of the child's shrunken pupils.

"Thanks."

Hurrying into the phone booth, she dropped a coin in the slot and, after consulting the identification card, dialed. Before the third ring a male voice with a Scandinavian accent said, "Mrs. Vandering's residence."

"May I speak to Mrs. Vandering?"

"Who is calling, please?"

"My name is Stacey—Ellen Stacey. Please tell her it's about her little girl." She added swiftly, "The little girl's— all right. I mean, she hasn't been in an accident."

"One moment, please."

Seconds later she heard a woman's voice, sharp with tension. "Yes?"

"Mrs. Vandering?"

"Yes! What's this about my daughter?"

"She's up at the Cloisters. I—found her here."

"What do you mean—found her?" The voice went high and thin. "Lindquist said she hadn't been hurt—"

Just how, Ellen wondered bleakly, do you tell another woman a thing like this about her child? "She seems to have taken some sort of drug, Mrs. Vandering. Heroin, I think. I found it in her purse. It's still there."

"Oh, God." It was a whimper. "Not again!" Then, after a pause: "Have you called anyone? The police, I mean?"

"No, I thought you wouldn't want—"

"Can you get a taxi?"

"I have one. But if you'd rather, I can wait here until you come for her."

After a moment the woman said distractedly, "No, you'd better bring her here."

"All right."

"Wait! Miss—Mrs.—"

"Miss Stacey. Ellen Stacey."

"Am I doing the right thing?" The voice was pleading. "I mean, you're all right, aren't you?"

All right. Not a kidnaper. Not a blackmailer, or a psycho, or any of the other dangerous persons into whose hands the helpless child might have fallen. "I'm all right, Mrs. Vandering. I'll get your daughter to you as fast as I can."

"You have the address?"

"Yes. It's on her identification card."

"Hurry. Please hurry." There was a click.

As they rode out of the parking lot, Ellen allowed the girl to huddle undisturbed in one corner of the seat. In a few minutes, Cecily would be no responsibility of hers. There would be others to ask the anguished questions—her doctor, and her parents. Or was it parent? "Mrs. Vandering's residence," the servant had said.

It was the child who broke the silence. Soon after they turned onto the Hudson River Parkway, she said in a whisper that sounded both frightened and hopeful, "Amy?"

Ellen, who had been staring at the river, turned her head.

"My name's not Amy. It's Ellen, Ellen Stacey."

Confusion now in the gray eyes with their contracted pupils. And then a leap of fear. "You'd better stay away from me," she whispered, "or they'll get you like they did Amy."

That was drugged nonsense, of course. Nevertheless, the child's voice held such hushed horror that Ellen felt a chill ripple down her back. "That's—" she began sharply, and broke off. She had been about to say that it was silly. "Who's Amy?"

"She was my friend. So they killed her."

For a moment as she looked down into the small face, Ellen had a sense of entering the gray world where the drugged child wandered. A lonely, hallucinated world where someone could become her friend only at peril of death. Ellen shuddered. Why had this eleven-year-old— apparently beloved, apparently in more than comfortable circumstances—chosen such a world?

Cecily was beginning to nod again. The long-lashed eyelids slowly closed. Once more Ellen felt the stab of an old, almost unbearable anguish. Beth used to look like that as she was falling asleep. Beth, who by now would have been only two years younger than this child.

She said, aware that she herself didn't believe it, "You're going to be all right, Cecily."

two

The elevator, smooth and noiseless and paneled with satiny dark wood, let them out on the twelfth floor. For a moment, until the elevator door closed with a whispering sound, Ellen sensed the operator's curious gaze fastened on their backs.

Evidently Mrs. Vandering's was the only twelfth-floor apartment served by that elevator, because a single door opened off the little square hallway, with its deep red carpet, its wall mirror reflecting two oriental vases set on a marble shelf. Her arm around Cecily's thin shoulders, Ellen crossed to the door and pressed the pearl button set in its frame.

Almost instantly the door opened. Looking at the small, fine-boned woman who stood there, Ellen found the comparison inevitable: she was like a camellia just beginning to turn brown at the edges. Her age was probably a year or two short of forty, although Ellen was sure that the well-kept face, when it didn't hold its present anguish, looked not much past thirty. She had hair of that expensive champagne color, delicate features, and lovely blue eyes with faint lines at the corners. Right now her eyes were wide with shock. Crouching, she drew her daughter to her, and placed her cheek against the dark curls. Neither responding nor resisting, the child stood motionless in her mother's arms.

The woman got to her feet. "Please come in, Miss Stacey. I'm Janet Vandering."

Ellen followed the woman and Cecily across a foyer into a living room. Midafternoon sunlight silhouetted the tall, portly figure of a man who stood looking through one of the long windows set in the west wall. He turned, and Mrs. Vandering said, "Miss Stacey, this is Dr. Carson."

Good, Ellen thought, as she greeted him. Mrs. Vandering had lost no time in summoning medical help.

Mrs. Vandering asked, "Will you excuse us for a few minutes, Miss Stacey?"

"Of course."

"Please sit down."

When the three of them had left the room, Ellen sank onto a straight chair upholstered in pale yellow satin. She looked around her at the Aubusson carpet on the dark parquet floor, and at the eighteenth-century French furniture which, if it were genuine, must be worth a fortune.

All this, and yet the child . . . Why?

Well, probably there was no one wise enough to answer that. Men might learn to live on the outer planets, and still not be able to say why one child, or adult, chose to retreat into a drug haze, while others in far worse circumstances were able to face unblurred reality.

Five minutes passed. Ten. A door opened and Mrs. Vandering came back into the room. Her face was still pale, but some of the tension had left it. "Sorry to have taken so long, Miss Stacey. We've put Cecily to bed for a little

10

while." She paused. "May I offer you a drink? Or could I make you a cup of tea? The servants are out at the moment."

She must have sent them away, Ellen reflected, so that they would not witness her child's return. "No, thank you. I must be going soon."

Sitting down on a satin-upholstered love seat, Mrs. Vandering clasped narrow hands in her lap. "First of all, I want to thank you for what you did."

Ellen murmured an acknowledgment.

"I suppose you're wondering—" She broke off, and then started again. "I mean, you're entitled to some explanation of what I said on the phone."

Ellen remembered that whimpering cry: "Oh, God! Not again!" She said, "Please don't explain anything you don't want to, Mrs. Vandering."

Mrs. Vandering's clasped hands tightened. Ellen could guess the nature of her indecision. Now that Cecily was, for the moment, safe, her mother had begun to worry about publicity. Would it be best to tell the stranger who had found her child as little as possible? Or would it be best to enlist her sympathy and, hopefully, her silence?

"As I suppose you gathered," she said, "this isn't Cecily's —first experience." Anger came into her voice. "I blame my brother-in-law—or rather, my ex-brother-in-law, since Cecily's father and I are divorced—for starting the whole thing. Nearly three years ago, soon after her ninth birthday, she and her father went to her uncle's studio one afternoon. We didn't find out until later, but when she came away she had half a dozen marijuana cigarettes with her."

Ellen said incredulously, "You can't mean that her uncle—?"

11

"No, of course not. He didn't give them to her. She found them in a jar in the kitchen while the two men were talking. Leonard—that's her uncle—said he doesn't smoke marijuana, and maybe he doesn't. He says some friend of his must have left them there. But what I blame him for is his carelessness. If it hadn't been for that, Cecily might never have—"

She broke off, but Ellen knew what she meant. Otherwise Cecily might not have learned, at a too-early age, to handle the knowledge that there are ways of making reality waver, and grow dim, and even disappear.

At last Ellen said into the silence, "But there's quite a difference between marijuana and hard drugs."

"I know." Her voice sounded tired. After a moment she went on, "As far as we've been able to discover, her first experience with heroin was last March. I was in Mexico then. I had arranged for a cousin of mine to stay here with Cecily while I was gone. When I got back, she seemed pale and listless, so I took her to Dr. Carson immediately."

"And he recognized the symptoms?"

The pale blond head nodded. "He finally got her to admit it. But we never learned where she'd gotten the drugs. All she gave us was an absurd story about finding an envelope filled with heroin—under a bush in Central Park!"

"Then you have no idea—?"

"Of course we have. She got the drug the way all children do—from some schoolmate."

"But doesn't she go to the Mainwaring School? I always thought it was excellent."

"No school is safe these days, Miss Stacey. The headmistress at Cecily's school became quite huffy when I told her about it. Later she said she had made a discreet investigation, and was convinced that Cecily hadn't obtained heroin from any of her other pupils." She hesitated. "Did Cecily tell you anything?"

"Yes. When I asked her who sold it to her, she said, 'I don't buy it. They give it to me.'"

"Which is about as silly," Mrs. Vandering said wearily, "as the Central Park bush story."

"I suppose so." Ellen hesitated. "But she did seem frightened. And I got the impression that it was the sort of fear she would have of adults, rather than children."

Mrs. Vandering shook her head emphatically. The idea that her daughter might be involved with adult traffickers in drugs obviously was insupportable to her. "Of course it's some other child, or children. And of course she must have paid them. Before I went to Mexico last year, I left her several weeks' allowance. Besides—"

Ellen waited.

"Besides, I've missed things around the apartment. Oh, nothing of great value. Crystal ashtrays, some coffee spoons, things like that. Perhaps it's the Lindquists, the couple I employ. I know Lindquist plays the races. But I haven't accused them because good help is so hard to find these days. And too—"

After a moment Ellen asked, "You thought it might be Cecily who took those things?"

The blue eyes were wretched. "Yes. She's become a stranger. My own child, and she's a stranger."

Straightening her shoulders, she went on in a firmer tone, "Now, Miss Stacey, Cecily's father, as you probably know, belongs to a very prominent family. If the newspapers—"

On the small gilt table at one end of the love seat, a phone rang. Mrs. Vandering glanced at Ellen, hesitated, and then said, "Excuse me." She picked up the phone. "Hello."

"Janet?" The masculine voice was so aggressively loud that Ellen, sitting only a few feet away, could hear it clearly.

"Oh, hello, Dale." Mrs. Vandering's voice, although pleasant, held an impatient undertone. "Please forgive me, but I'm afraid I can't talk to you right now."

"Forgive you. *Forgive* you! That's a tall order, Janet."

Mrs. Vandering didn't answer that. Feeling her face flush with embarrassment, Ellen turned and gazed at the painting hung above the marble-manteled fireplace, a portrait of a younger and even lovelier Mrs. Vandering. Did her hostess realize that the caller's voice was audible several feet away? If so, she must be wishing she had taken the call on some other phone.

Mrs. Vandering broke the short silence. "I'm sorry, Dale, but I must hang up now."

"Oh, no, you don't. If you do, I'll keep calling. Or I'll come up to see you. I'm right in the neighborhood."

"Dale, please understand. It's quite imposs—"

"I understand, all right! You've decided now that you don't even want to see me. And you expect me to crawl off into the bushes and keep quiet, like a nice little gentleman." The voice thickened. "I broke up my marriage for you, Janet. I gave up my children. Visitation rights! I get to see them two lousy afternoons a month. And now you think I'll let you—"

"I really must hang up." Her tone had hardened. "I have a visitor."

"Who? A man? Some other poor fool who thinks he's going to marry you? Or is the shoe on the other foot this time? Maybe you're the one who—"

"Good-by, Dale. It was nice to talk to you." Ellen, still gazing at the portrait, heard a click.

After a moment Mrs. Vandering said, "Sorry for the interruption. Now what were we saying?"

Turning her head, Ellen saw that her hostess's face was calm. Aware that her own face must still hold embarrassment, she felt wry admiration for the other woman's poise. Social training over stage training, she thought, by a knockout. "I believe you were going to ask me—not to discuss your daughter with anyone."

"Yes. I'd be eternally grateful if you kept the whole matter confidential. So would Howard—Cecily's father, I mean. Ugly publicity could ruin the child's whole life."

"I see no reason why I should mention it to anyone."

"Thank you." She paused. "May I ask you a little about yourself, Miss Stacey? What do you do, for instance?"

"I'm an actress."

"Oh. A stage actress?"

Did that fleeting look of dismay mean that Mrs. Vandering thought that an actress couldn't be depended upon to keep a confidence? Or was it that in New York "actress" and "model" were sometimes euphuisms for a less reputable calling?

"I've been in off-Broadway shows, and summer stock. I do quite a few TV commercials. And occasionally I have small parts in movies made here in New York."

Mrs. Vandering's smile was nicely in place now. "It must be very interesting."

"Sometimes it is. Mrs. Vandering, what will happen to Cecily now?"

Mrs. Vandering didn't frown, but something in her tone

15

conveyed that she thought the question unnecessary. "Dr. Carson has a small private clinic. She'll stay there for a while. About a week should suffice. After all, it's not as if she were really an—addict."

Perhaps not, Ellen thought, but if this happened a few more times . . .

She recalled Cecily in the cab, dark-lashed eyelids closing just as Beth's used to against the faint glow of the night light beside her railed bed.

"Mrs. Vandering, may I see Cecily again? After she's well?"

Shades seemed to come down in the lovely blue eyes. "Oh, I'm afraid—I mean, would that really be wise, Miss Stacey? To remind the child of all this? Oh, it isn't that I'm not grateful, extremely grateful. In fact, if there was some way to express—"

Her gaze went to an exquisitely burnished alligator handbag on the little table beside the phone.

Ellen had felt sympathy for Cecily's mother, and admiration of her self-control. Now, for the first time, she felt dislike.

She must have betrayed herself by some stiffening of her face or body, because Mrs. Vandering said swiftly, "But I realize there just isn't any way to express it. All I can do is to say thank you. And, of course, pay for the cab that brought you here."

Ellen said evenly, "Thank you." After all, if she hadn't encountered Cecily, she would have taken the bus home. "I had to pay the driver waiting time. It came to three-fifty, with the tip."

She took the three bills and the silver Mrs. Vandering

16

handed to her, said thank you, and rose. "I must go home now."

Mrs. Vandering accompanied her to the door. "I'm not only grateful for all you've done, Miss Stacey. I'm grateful for your promise to keep this confidential."

So she was still worrying about that. Well, who could blame her? She couldn't know that Ellen, for special and private reasons, felt more than a stranger's concern for the dazed child she had found. "I'll keep that promise, Mrs. Vandering."

A minute or so later, emerging from the elevator into the spacious lobby, she saw that the doorman was busy. He stood out on the sidewalk, facing a thin, red-haired man. To judge by their gestures, the men were arguing. She pushed open the plate glass door.

"—imperative that I see Mrs. Vandering. Absolutely imperative."

It was the voice of the man on the phone. One rapid glance told Ellen that he appeared to be in his late thirties, and that his haircut and clothing probably had been obtained on Madison Avenue.

"I'm sorry, Mr. Haylock. Mrs. Vandering left strict orders."

As Ellen turned to her left along the wide sidewalk, she heard the red-haired man say, "But you don't understand. This is vitally important."

What had Mrs. Vandering called him? Dale? Dale Haylock, then—a man who had cut himself off from his children for Janet Vandering's sake, only to be jilted by her.

Dale Haylock. Janet Vandering and her ex-husband. Drug-dazed Cecily. With every material advantage, ap-

17

parently, they had all four made a sad hash of their lives. Suddenly her own lonely, economically precarious existence looked good to her. Straightening her shoulders a little, she moved on through the cold sunshine.

three

Seated at the mahogany desk in his eighteenth-floor office, his gaze fixed on the George Bingham landscape on the paneled wall opposite, Howard Vandering thought, not for the first time, "What am I doing here?"

He knew that to others the question would sound absurd. He was here because this was the office of the president of Vandering Enterprises, and that was who he was, the president.

Yes, but why had he founded Vandering Enterprises?

Why hadn't he been content, like three generations of Vanderings before him, to let others manage the fortune accumulated, early in the nineteenth century, by old Samuel Vandering?

Janet had foretold his present predicament that afternoon eight years ago, a few hours after his father's funeral. There in the Fifth Avenue apartment, surrounded by the exquisite French furniture that seemed the perfect background for her delicate beauty, she had asked, "Why are you doing this? It's not as if you're an idler. You're a Yale trustee, you're on the museum board, and the opera board. And now you'll take your father's place in the Vandering

Foundation—"

"I want to make a place of my own." He might have added that he wanted to see if, after four generations, the Vandering strain still held some of old Samuel's tough shrewdness. Samuel, illiterate until the age of fifteen, who had won an Erie Canal barge in a probably crooked poker game, hired thugs to terrorize the crews of other barges until their owners sold out to him, and then traded the barges for railroad stock. By the time of his death in the eighteen-seventies he had accumulated, if not one of the great American fortunes, at least one of the second rank.

He hadn't thought it best to mention Samuel to Janet, though. She had none of Howard's sneaking admiration for his ancestor. To her old Samuel was nothing more or less than a thieving, bullying scoundrel.

"What leads you to think," Janet asked, "that at the age of forty you can take the financial world by storm?"

Howard's jaw tightened. "My work on various boards involves financial matters. And I had business training in college."

"Almost twenty years ago!"

He asked, after a moment, "Is it that you think I'm not bright enough, or too soft?"

"Oh, Howard! What have you ever had to make you tough? Do you know what's wrong with you? You're envious of Leonard. Just because he's done something on his own, you feel you have to."

There was some truth in that, Howard had admitted silently. It was galling to think that his half-brother, at only twenty-five, was a recognized painter, with canvases hanging at the Museum of Modern Art and in private collections, and with enough income from his work to support the

20

rackety sort of life he led.

"If you're determined to buy these companies," Janet went on, "I hope you won't use all your money."

"Of course not. The bulk of it will remain invested in tax-exempt bonds, just as it has always been."

"Good. I don't expect you to be overly concerned about me." Their eyes, meeting, had acknowledged the growing coldness between them—a coldness that was to lead them to the divorce court two years later. "But you have your daughter to think of."

Cecily.

Getting up from his desk, he crossed the thick beige carpet to stand at the window. Through the glass wall of a building about twenty feet away, he could see two shirt-sleeved men, bathed in a fluorescent glare as they bent over a drafting table.

Cecily. Now that Amy Thornhill was dead, his daughter remained the only living person that he really loved.

Oh, he had loved Janet when he married her. But sexually their lives together, from the very first, had been strained, unsatisfactory. In the fourth year of their marriage, by mutual, though tacit, consent, he was leaving her undisturbed in her bedroom and turning elsewhere.

Unlike Amy, who came into his life after the divorce, the girls he had known during those years had meant little or nothing to him. He couldn't even remember the name of the girl who, if it had been a New York divorce, would have been the corespondent. Marlene? Maureen?

Anyway, he could remember her last name. Closky. Not McClosky. Just Closky. Janet's detectives had tracked them to that Pennsylvania hotel, and for a few minutes it had been pretty ugly, the girl huddling there with the sheet

21

drawn up to her neck, and the two detective creeps alternating between spurious self-righteousness and equally spurious man-to-man sympathy.

Not, he was sure, that Janet had wanted to drag him through a New York divorce court. But the threat was there. And never mind that he suspected that she too had turned elsewhere. To Dale Haylock, for instance, that blue-blooded ex-tennis bum who these days was crying into his martinis all over town because Janet had changed her mind about marrying him.

No, all that mattered was that Howard had got caught, and she hadn't. Before she left for Reno, he had promised, in writing, never to contest her custody of their daughter. He had also, in lieu of alimony, settled two million on her, and signed over the deed to the Fifth Avenue cooperative apartment. Consequently she'd been able to live much as she had before the divorce.

Cecily was the one who had been hurt. Why had she been hurt so much? Hell, half of his friends had been divorced at least once. Their kids seemed to adjust. But maybe it was like hemophilia. Some injury that meant nothing to a normal child could kill a bleeder. Maybe, emotionally speaking, his daughter was a bleeder.

The worst part was that as time went on the damage she had sustained in the crash of her parents' marriage seemed to grow more severe, rather than less so. Right after the divorce, when she first began to spend the allotted two weekends a month at his apartment, she had seemed unable to comprehend the permanency of her parents' separation. Perhaps that wasn't surprising. She had been only six then. "When you come back to live with us, Daddy" she would say, "I'll hang my elephant picture in your room." Or teach

22

you to play Old Maid. Or bake cookies for you in my little electric stove.

Gently, he would remind her that he wasn't coming back. "Oh, yes," she would say, "you told me." But from the hope in her eyes he could tell she didn't believe him.

It had taken about a year for the hope to die out of her face. Gradually, during those twice-monthly weekends, he had become aware that his daughter was now too quiet, too polite. The Plaza for lunch? Yes, Daddy, if you want to. The circus, the children's ballet? Yes, Daddy, that would be nice.

But the circus clowns could never elicit more than a polite little smile from her. And once at the ballet he had seen her staring at the Wicked Witch, not with the half-gleeful apprehension on the other young faces around them, but with a look of brooding horror. What, he'd wondered, did the witch mean to her? Some specific person? Or just the bleakness of her inner world?

On the desk behind him, the intercom buzzed. Turning, he flipped the switch. "Yes, Miss Morrison?"

"I wondered if you noticed that pre-publication copy of the tool company's annual report. I put it on your desk while you were out to lunch."

"Yes, thank you. I was just about to read it." He released the switch. Or maybe he wouldn't read it, he thought, looking down at the report's blue cover. He already knew what was in it. Bad news. Returning to the window, he again stared at the draftsmen in the building opposite.

It was his increasing worry over his daughter, he felt convinced, that had brought about his business reverses. Vandering Enterprises had done fairly well during its first two years of existence. Sure, some people might say that everybody had been making money in the mid-sixties. But he knew that he'd had more going for him than a favorable economic climate. In those days he had made the right decisions more often than not. It was only after he became seriously depressed over his daughter's continuing unhappiness that he began to make bad mistakes—the wrong men hired for executive spots, a disastrous investment in a Canadian oil outfit, an expansion of the Florida pre-fab company only months before the new administration had tightened up on mortgage money.

Almost three years ago, when Cecily had just turned nine, there had been that marijuana business. Unlike his ex-wife, Howard didn't blame his brother Leonard for that. According to Len—and Howard believed him—he'd had no idea that some whimsical visitor to his loft apartment-studio had stashed a half dozen joints in a cookie jar in the kitchen. "If I had," he'd said, an unhappy frown on his handsome face, "and if I'd had any idea Cecily would find them, I'd have thrown them out before you got here that day."

Cecily had promised Howard and her mother that she would never smoke marijuana again, and he felt, although he couldn't be sure, that she had kept that promise. For a while after that his world seemed to take a turn for the better. He had met Dan Reardon, tough, likable Dan, with his easy grin that seemed to contradict his reputation as the latest financial whiz kid—and eventually had persuaded the younger man to join Vandering Enterprises. And he had met Amy Thornhill, executive secretary to one of his business associates.

Amy was thirty-five, and a spinster. Until two years before, when death had relieved her of the obligation, she had been the sole support of her mother. Amy had a face that was nice-looking rather than pretty, and a figure a little too broad in the hips to be fashionable. But she also had good sense leavened with humor, and poise combined with a gentle warmth. Before Howard had known her a month, he was far more deeply in love with her than he had ever been with Janet.

To Howard's delight, Cecily took to Amy at once, and in the young woman's presence became almost a chatterbox. Soon Amy was taking Cecily to shops and to matinees, not just on the weekends she spent at her father's Central Park South apartment, but on other Saturdays too. Janet—perhaps because she was busy with her friends, perhaps because she was glad that her withdrawn little daughter had found someone to whom she could respond—made no objection to these excursions. After Janet had left for Mexico a year ago last March, Amy and Cecily had seen even more of each other.

It was late on a Saturday afternoon, ten days after Janet's departure for Mexico, that Amy had phoned him at his apartment. "Howard, are you free for an hour or so? I'd like to talk to you about something."

He had answered reluctantly, "Amy, I can't. I'm due at the Roosevelt right now. Dan Reardon and I are having drinks and dinner with those two men from Arden Camera. They've flown here from Chicago." Although in the end the negotiations with Arden had come to nothing, they had seemed important at the time, a fact that Amy knew. "Can't you tell me what it is over the phone?"

"No," she said, after a moment, "it would take too long. Besides, you've got this Arden business on your mind. I'll see you tomorrow."

"At least tell me whether or not you're all right."

"I'm fine."

"Then is it something about Cecily?"

Her hesitation was so brief that he might have imagined it. "She's fine, too. We had lunch at the cafeteria in the park, and then went to the zoo. I left her at her apartment house half an hour ago. It's nothing that can't wait. So enjoy your dinner, darling, and good luck."

He didn't talk to her again, nor see her—not alive. Sometime after midnight that night, two men—the police said there must have been two of them—broke into her apartment, shot her through the temple as she lay in bed, and, apparently, took whatever money they found in her purse and whatever valuables that had been in her desk or bureau. Their haul couldn't have amounted to much. Howard had meant to give her jewelry—an engagement diamond, and rubies for her ears and throat—but he hadn't gotten around to it yet, and so the most valuable ornament she had owned was an opal ring which had belonged to her mother. Thus his grief had held a special bitterness. The thieves couldn't have netted more than a couple of hundred dollars for their night's work. And for that they had killed her.

Amy's death obviously had been a blow to his small daughter, too. She had grown even more thin and quiet and listless. And then, returning from Mexico, Janet had made the discovery that the child had been sniffing heroin.

After the initial stunned horror, his first reaction had been to blame Janet. Why had she stayed in Mexico almost six weeks? But he couldn't evade the knowledge that both of them had failed their too-vulnerable child. Somehow, he and Janet should have managed to stay together. He'd even proposed remarriage. Janet had rejected the idea. If it

26

hadn't worked before, it would work even less well now, to Cecily's detriment as well as their own. Nor would she consider taking Cecily to a psychiatrist. If psychiatrists were so good at straightening people out, she said, why should they themselves have the highest suicide rate of any professional group? No, she herself could give Cecily close companionship, if that was what was needed. She would take her to Europe right away, and keep her there until late July. When they returned, Cecily would study with a tutor, so that despite her missed schoolwork, she could re-enter Mainwaring in the fall.

Well, the prescription had seemed to work. Not that a few months of travel had turned Cecily into a bubbling extrovert. But she had come back from Europe a couple of pounds heavier, and she'd retained that weight through the winter. What was more, her mid-semester report card in April had been good.

Over in the fluorescent-lighted drafting room, the draftsmen had begun to make just-before-quitting-time motions. One was putting on his coat. The other was folding over the outspread blueprints. Howard looked at his watch. Twenty of five. Reluctantly he decided that he had better at least look at that report.

He had just sat down at the desk when his phone rang, the one with an outside line and an unlisted number.

It was Janet, her voice taut. "Something awful's happened to Cecily."

His heart seemed to stop for a moment, and then began to pound. "Janet, for God's sake—"

"It's—heroin again. She was found up at the Cloisters."

When he could speak, he asked, "Where is she now?"

"Dr. Carson's taken her to the clinic. They just left here."

"Did the police—?"

"No, a girl found her and brought her home."

"What girl?"

"Just a girl," Janet said impatiently. "Some actress I never heard of. Her name is Ellen Stacey. She promised not to talk, but just the same I'm worried. She seemed too interested in Cecily, even wanted to see her again."

How typical of Janet. Distressed as she was over their child, she could still worry about the relatively minor matter of a possible scandal.

"Do you want me to come to your apartment?"

"No, thanks, Howard. Cousin Martha will spend the night here."

Martha Barlow, her mother's cousin. Of course, he thought numbly. Mrs. Barlow, plain, widowed, and fifty, was that invaluable asset, a poor relation who was always available.

"Then I'll go straight to the clinic."

"Dr. Carson doesn't want either of us there tonight. We can talk to her on the phone tomorrow, and perhaps see her in a few days."

"How long—?"

"He plans to keep her there until Saturday, not for medical reasons so much as to try to find out where she got the drug. She isn't in a bad way physically. I mean"— the words came out painfully—"it's not as if she'd been injecting the stuff."

"Oh, God! Why? Why does it have to be our child?"

Her voice was high and sharp. "What's the use of asking a question like that? There's the doorbell. It must be Cousin Martha. Good-by, Howard."

He went on sitting there, dimly aware that the room,

shadowed by taller buildings surrounding this one, was growing dark, until the intercom's buzz aroused him. His hand felt heavy as he reached out and flipped the switch. "Yes?"

"Mr. Reardon is here."

"Send him in."

"Is it all right if I leave now, Mr. Vandering? It's past five."

"Yes. Good night, Miss Morrison."

The door opened and Dan Reardon walked in. "Hi."

Howard nodded.

"Thought you'd like to know that the plastic container deal looks good. They've shaved their price ten percent, which means we can put more into expansion. That is, if we decide we want the company."

Howard said, with an effort, "We'll see."

"I suppose you've heard the closing prices. Flying Squirrel up a full point." That was Dan's name for the small airline that had been Vandering Enterprises' first acquisition. "And on heavy volume, too."

"Who were the suckers buying?"

"Nobody in particular. Most of the buying was in odd lots, and in street names. But I'm not sure they're suckers. I think we can pull that company into the black, Howard, if we feed a little more capital into it. Incidentally, why the hell are we talking in the dark like this?"

There was a click. Scone lights bloomed along the walls. Howard stared dully at his junior partner. Dan Reardon, the Tough Mick, as Howard secretly thought of him. Thirty-seven, and looking younger. Dark curly hair, deep blue eyes, and blunt features, permanently tanned. An expensively tailored suit which, like Dan's own personality, displayed a defiant touch of up-from-the-slums flamboyance in its slightly widened lapels.

Dan said in a completely altered tone, "Howard, for God's sake, what's happened?"

"My little girl—" His throat closed up.

After a moment Dan said, "She isn't—?"

"No, she's not hurt."

Again Dan waited for the older man to go on. Finally he asked, "Same business as last spring?"

"Yes."

Sitting down in one of the red leather armchairs, Dan fixed his gaze at a point on the opposite wall, and said nothing. Howard looked at him gratefully. When it really counted, Dan could be more tactful than most of the men Howard had grown up with.

But it wasn't because of his tact that Howard had broached the idea of a partnership that day nearly two years ago in the steamroom of the Midtown Club. It had been because he felt that if anyone could get Vandering Enterprises back on its feet, Reardon could.

Like many of his fellow members, Howard had been surprised when Dan Reardon was admitted to that Ivy League bastion, the Midtown Club. A native of the depressed Brooklyn area known as Red Hook, Dan had left Brooklyn College in his sophomore year to become a securities salesman. Intelligent and brash and lucky, he had made enough in the long bull market to switch to conglomerates before he was thirty. By the time he decided to join the Midtown Club—"I heard you served the best food in town," he later told Howard—he had a sufficient reputation as a financial wizard, and had put enough men in his debt, that it was easy for him to obtain the required seven sponsors.

30

Howard had felt drawn to the younger man's personality, with its combination of toughness, shrewdness, and, when the need for it arose, almost reckless daring. Soon he found himself telling Dan things he wouldn't have discussed with his older associates. His anxieties about his daughter, for instance, and his financial worries. Finally, one day in the Midtown's steamroom, Howard had broached the idea of Dan joining Vandering Enterprises.

A frown had creased Dan's sweating forehead. "As a full partner?"

"If those are your terms."

After a while Dan said, "In the first place, I've got fish of my own to fry. In the second place—now don't get sore, Howard—from what I hear you're in even worse shape than you've said. Just offhand, I'd say you should unload some of your companies, for whatever you can get. In the case of others, you ought to go public, and then expand."

"Sell stock? I've liked keeping control—"

"Better forty percent control of a growing concern than a hundred percent of a bomb. Or, if you want to in the case of some of the outfits—now just tell me if I'm out of line, Howard—haven't you got enough of the gilt-edged stuff in reserve that you could finance necessary expansion yourself?"

Howard nodded.

"Well, you could do it that way if you want, although personally I like stockholders in there to share the risk. Anyway, I think that a program of dumping some companies and expanding others would work. Not right away, but eventually."

"We can discuss details later. Right now, how about that partnership?"

31

"I'll have to think it over. Give me until tomorrow, huh?"

The next day he had phoned. "It's a deal, provided I can come in as a junior partner. I've decided I want to keep on running some of my own outfits, at least the mutual funds. That means I can't give Vandering Enterprises full time. But if I can come in as a junior partner—"

Howard said, with vast relief, "You can."

Under Dan's guidance, Vandering Enterprises had done a little better. Not a great deal. As Dan had said, it would be a long haul. The tool company was floundering, despite an infusion of stockholder money and some of Howard's own. But other firms that might have gone under had at least survived. Still others were making a little money.

Now Dan said into the silence, "You want to talk about your kid, or shall I get out?"

It was an effort to speak. "There's not much to tell. Some actress by the name of Eleanor Stacey found her. No, I think Janet said Ellen. Anyway, she found Cecily at the Cloisters and brought her home."

"The Cloisters. My God. Next thing they'll be pushing the stuff in St. Patrick's Cathedral." He paused. "Did you say the girl who found her was an actress?"

Howard wasn't deceived by the younger man's casual tone. In financial circles, Dan's interest in spectacular— and expensive—women was a source of half-disapproving, half-envious gossip.

"Yes. I'm afraid Janet wasn't very nice to her. She said the girl seemed too interested in Cecily, even wanted to see her again. I suppose she meant after—after Cecily's well."

"Have you seen her yet?"

"Cecily? No, she's at Dr. Carson's clinic. He thinks neither Janet nor I should see her for a few days."

32

"But I suppose you'll want to stick around town."

Howard asked heavily, "Why?"

"Well, I thought that while you're waiting to see your kid, maybe you'd like to go out to Toledo and take a look at the tool factory."

Here was more of that instinctive tact, Howard felt, under the wheeler-dealer exterior. Howard could accomplish nothing at all by a trip to Toledo, and both men knew it. But at least it would offer him distraction while he waited to see his daughter.

"I might do that. Day after tomorrow, say."

"Well, think it over." He rose.

When the door had closed behind Dan, Howard stared at the phone on his desk, the one with an outside line. Call Leonard? Yes, he was Cecily's uncle. He had a right to know what had happened to her.

Drawing the phone to him, he dialed.

four

At the corner of Fifth Avenue and Sixty-eighth Street, Ellen hesitated. Her own walkup apartment was still more than five blocks away, on Sixty-fifth Street between Lexington and Third Avenues. But the Mainwaring school, if she remembered rightly from her walks around the neighborhood, was on Sixty-eighth. Impulsively, she turned to her left.

Midway of the block between Madison and Park Avenues, she slowed her footsteps. Yes, here it was, a tall brownstone about eighty years old, to judge by the bay windows bulging from its first floor. She paused for a moment, looking at the highly polished brass nameplate, and at the ilex trees, set in tubs, which flanked the double front door.

"Excuse me, but does your daughter attend this school?"

Ellen turned. The woman who stood beside her, tall and elegantly thin, appeared to be in her late seventies. She wore a classically simple navy blue coat and, upon her white hair, a navy pillbox trimmed with artificial violets.

Despite a twinge of pain, Ellen smiled. "I have no daughter."

"But you know someone who has a daughter enrolled here?"

"Yes, slightly." Odd, she thought. This woman didn't look like the sort who would accost a stranger with personal questions. Ellen smiled again and turned away.

To her surprise, the old lady fell into step beside her. "You see, I'm interested in the school. In fact, I live in the next block, and I walk past here several times a day." She paused. "I'm Amanda Mainwaring."

"Mainwaring! Was the school named after your family?"

"It was named after me. I founded it." The face she turned to Ellen had changed. A spot of color burned on each cheekbone, and the faded blue eyes were bright. "My niece forced me out five years ago. My own niece! She and the trustees said that I had become incompetent."

Ellen said, embarrassed, "I'm sorry."

"Oh, you needn't feel sorry for me!" She laughed. "You'd better be sorry for my niece. Things have gone wrong lately. Is it because of the Vandering child that you were looking at the school?"

The question had come so swiftly and unexpectedly that Ellen said, before she could check herself, "Why, how on earth—"

"How did I know?" The old face smiled, not pleasantly. "Oh, I learn things. There are a few people at the school who are still loyal to me. For instance, I know that the Vandering child was found with drugs in her possession over a year ago. And I know that Mrs. Vandering, very upset, phoned my niece this afternoon to say that some young woman had found the child up at the Cloisters today, half-unconscious. So when I saw you, a young woman I had never seen before, staring at the school, I thought that

35

perhaps—"

Who was Amanda Mainwaring's informant? One of the teachers? A member of the office staff? Some domestic worker who supplied the needs the boarding pupils? Aside from the matter of disloyalty to the school, it seemed unlikely that anyone would risk her job by spying for an embittered old woman. And yet how else could Amanda Mainwaring have known that, earlier this afternoon, a drug-dazed Cecily Vandering had been found up at the Cloisters?

They had reached the corner of Park Avenue. "And I was right, wasn't I?" The old woman's hand, surprisingly strong in its spotless white kid glove, gripped Ellen's arm, bringing her to a halt. "You are the one who found the Vandering girl. Does that sound as if I've grown stupid and incompetent? Does it?"

"No, of course not." Not stupid. But perhaps more than a little mad. "Excuse me, Mrs. Mainwaring."

"Miss Mainwaring."

"Excuse me, but I turn off here."

A little after ten that night, Ellen took off her robe and slipped into bed. Lifting the Helen Hayes autobiography from the night table, she held it, unopened, in her hand.

There had been a message for her when she phoned her answering service: Please call your agent.

Her agent, a woman, had two pieces of news for her. On the following afternoon Ellen would have a chance to compete for the wife's role in a TV coffee commercial. And, if she chose to, she could work Wednesday night on a movie being made by some outfit called McClellan Films. "It's not much, dear," the agent said apologetically. "No lines. But they'll be shooting at other locations in New

York—a Brooklyn skating rink, for instance—and so if you're a nice, cooperative girl you might get four or five days' more work on this picture."

Four or five days. Enough to pay the rent. "I'm a nice, cooperative girl. Where and when?"

The agent gave an address on upper Broadway. "It's an old movie theater, not in use now. You're to wear a long white dress. Eight o'clock, Wednesday night."

Ellen didn't ask the title of the film, or what it was about, or who was starring in it. Her agent wouldn't know, and Ellen herself might not find out, even after she was on the set. She had collected many a day's pay without learning anything more than the film's production number, chalked on the clapboard.

Her answering service had received no message from Charles. On the whole, she had decided, she was relieved rather than disappointed. For some time now she'd had an uneasy feeling that her reasons for wanting to marry Charles—her frequent loneliness, and that thirtieth birthday looming up not too far ahead—were not adequate. True, there was still another reason. Some of his gestures, and certain tones of his voice, had reminded her of Richard. But that too would have been an inadequate reason for marrying him, because Charles wasn't Richard, and never could be.

When she was eighteen and a student at the Academy of Dramatic Arts, she had met a young photographer named Richard Stacey at a party one night. Three months later they were married.

Almost up until the birth of their child Beth, in the second year of their marriage, Ellen had continued her studies at the Academy. After Beth's arrival, of course,

37

Ellen could no longer be a full-time student, but she did manage to take lessons from a dramatic coach twice a week. Richard, who had been an advocate of Women's Liberation years before the term had been invented, approved of the lessons. "I don't want one of those frustrated wives," he had told her. "You've got talent, and if you don't use it, you'll be unhappy, and make Beth and me unhappy." When she began to get calls for TV commercials, he was both pleased and proud.

One mid-December afternoon, soon after Beth's second birthday, Ellen learned that she had been chosen as the second lead in an off-Broadway play—a role she had auditioned for so many weeks earlier that she had almost forgotten about it. Rehearsals were to begin immediately. Pleased and yet dismayed, she phoned Richard at his studio.

"I guess I'll have to turn it down."

"Turn it down! Are you crazy?"

"But it's almost Christmas. Mother and Dad will be heartbroken if we don't see them this year." The previous Christmas, Ellen had caught flu, and so they had been unable to fly to her family's home in southern California. "Just think, they haven't seen Beth since she was a week old."

"They'll see her. Beth and I will fly out there."

"But, Richard! To be separated at Christmastime!"

"It's up to you, honey. But I know how much you want that part. And you keep talking about a weekend place in the Poconos. If the play has a long run, maybe we could afford it."

A weekend place. Raised in sight of the Sierra Madres, Ellen was often homesick for the smell of pine needles and the blue sparkle of mountain lakes. "All right. I'll take it."

A few days before Christmas, Ellen skipped a rehearsal to accompany her husband and child to Kennedy Airport. She watched Richard carry Beth down the ramp to the plane. The little face under the dark curls, looking back over Richard's shoulder, had lost the pleased excitement it had worn all morning, and was beginning to pucker with the realization of something that she had been told, but apparently hadn't believed until now. Mama wasn't coming with them.

Feeling more than a little tearful herself, and yet grateful that she had a husband as lovingly cooperative as Richard, Ellen took the airport bus back to the city. It wasn't until she turned on the radio for the five o'clock news that she learned the plane had never left Kennedy. It had skidded on the runway, side-slipped, and burst into flames.

Of the seventy-odd passengers aboard, fourteen had lived. Neither Richard nor Beth was one of the fourteen.

Ellen had never even thought of that legendary tradition that the show must go on. Dazed and broken, she had gone to her parents' California house and remained there two months. Then, aware that she could not become her parents' young daughter again, even if she had wanted to, she had returned to New York City. Through an agency that specialized in shared rentals, she had met the young school-teacher who had been living in this apartment, and moved in with her. A few months later, the teacher had married. Since then Ellen had lived there alone.

And she had worked these past seven years. She had been a nurse, secretly in love with her doctor employer, in a TV soap opera. In commercials, she had rejoiced over an oven cleaner, soothed a cranky husband with tranquillizers, and plugged dozens of other products designed to keep the buyer happy, popular, and smelling like a rose. She probably worked at her profession more frequently than eighty percent of Actors Equity members. Only twice during those seven years had she found it necessary to take a stopgap job as a department store clerk.

And yet, except to people in show business and a few vacationers who attended the same summer theaters year after year, her name was unknown.

And by now it was likely to remain so. Perhaps if present-day playwrights wrote more starring roles like Candida and Hedda Gabler, roles for thirtyish actresses . . . But they didn't. These days, if you weren't old enough to play the lead in *Forty Carats,* you'd better be young enough to play the teen-ager in *The Chalk Garden.*

Why, then, had she persisted in a career that offered little recognition and only irregular income? Why had she turned down that law clerk who five years ago had wanted to marry her, and that TV cameraman who had proposed last summer? Why hadn't she tried harder to hold onto Charles? Married to him, she wouldn't have to worry when her answering service reported, "No messages." She wouldn't even have an answering service. Why, then?

She knew why. Every once in a while—walking off a TV set, or bowing to a straw-hat audience—she had a sense that she had done her very best, and that her best was pretty good. Not great, but more than just adequate. And those moments, seldom as they came, offered her more satisfaction than she felt she could obtain through marriage to a man she merely liked.

Besides, she thought with a smile, in another ten years, if she learned to sing and dance in the meantime, she might have a long and profitable career playing Dolly. Opening the Helen Hayes autobiography at the bookmark, she began to read.

On the stand beside her bed, the phone rang. Ellen laid down the book, reached out. "Hello."

"Miss Stacey?" The voice was soft, husky. "Or is it Mrs. Stacey?"

A telephone nut? Like many New York women living alone, Ellen had tried to escape the attention of such callers by having herself listed in the phone book as "E. B. Stacey." But some of the kooks who made such calls had caught onto that.

She asked sharply, "Who is this?"

"Never mind about me. Now about you. You're a healthy girl, aren't you?" She took the phone away from her ear. As if the movement had been visible over the wire, the caller said, more loudly, "Don't hang up! I've just one thing to say. If you want to stay healthy, mind your own business." There was a click.

Annoyed, Ellen replaced the phone in its cradle. If you want to stay healthy, mind your own business! Someone had been watching old gangster films—very old ones. But at least he'd been less upsetting than a previous caller who, as soon as she answered, launched into a series of the words compulsive small boys write on walls.

Or should she consider tonight's call less upsetting?

That pitiful child today, saying, "Leave me alone," and, later on, "You'd better stay away from me."

Absurd to think that the call of a moment ago lent any weight to the child's hallucinations. Cecily was just a sick little girl. And the man who had called was just a sadist, chuckling now over the woman he pictured quaking with fear—unless, of course, he was at this moment threatening some other woman.

Determinedly, she took up her book. But faces kept getting between her and the printed page. Cecily's, with the wideset gray eyes and pointed chin. Janet Vandering's Dresden-china face. Dale Haylock's, holding barely controlled rage as he argued with the doorman. Amanda Mainwaring's classic old face, suddenly flushed and glittering-eyed under the outmoded hat. And then she recalled something else—not a face, but the stocky silhouette of the man with whom she had bumped shoulders in a doorway at the Cloisters.

For the first time, she wondered if he could possibly have been the child's drug supplier. No, of course not. No pusher would hang around a customer, particularly in a public place, until the heroin had taken effect. Instead he'd hurry away the moment the sale was made.

Her thoughts returned to the phone caller. Had he been a man? She had assumed so. But if a woman pitched her voice low . . .

Annoyed with herself, she looked at the clock. Almost eleven. If she couldn't read, she had better try to sleep.

As soon as she turned off the light, there was Cecily's face, the long-lashed eyelids drooping as Beth's used to in the night light's glow. Abruptly Ellen sat up, turned on the bedside lamp, and with a grim expression, opened her book.

At one-thirty, she was still reading.

In the dream, the sleeper handed Cecily Vandering a transparent plastic packet. From it the child extracted a book of paper matches and walked over to a shingled building, perhaps a tool shed, that hadn't been in the dream until that moment. She struck a match and held it to a

42

shingle until the wood burst into flame. She held another lighted match to a shingle, and then another and another. Now the shed was a flaming torch. . . .

In the street several stories below, a car backfired. The sleeper awoke and, after a second or two, contemplated with a smile the apt symbolism of the dream. Not heroin in the envelope, but matches—matches with which a seemingly solid structure would be destroyed, like the flimsy, aging thing it was.

Still smiling, the awakened dreamer turned over in bed and went back to sleep.

five

Even the next day, Ellen couldn't escape thoughts of Cecily Vandering. As she dressed for the coffee commerical audition, she kept seeing the small white face, the gray eyes with their contracted pupils. And when she was actually on the set that afternoon, she found it hard to register sly feminine triumph over the fact that the actor playing her husband—a confirmed hater of instant coffee, according to the script—had asked for a second cup of the sponsor's coffee. Afterward, descending in the elevator, she thought dismally, "Well, I blew that one."

There was no help for it. She would have to involve herself with Cecily again, at least to the extent of finding out how she was today. Then, perhaps, she could keep her mind upon her own concerns. In a drugstore phone booth she looked up the Carson Clinic, and then dialed.

"You have a young patient named Cecily Vandering," she said a moment later. "Could you tell me how she is?"

"Who's calling, please?"

"My name is Stacey—Ellen Stacey."

"Please wait."

At least two minutes passed before the voice said, "I'm

sorry, but there must be some mistake. We have no patient of that name."

After a moment Ellen asked, "May I speak to Dr. Carson?"

The reply came promptly. "I'm sorry. Dr. Carson is out of town."

Ellen hung up. So the child had been made inaccessible behind the walls that money and influence can erect. And Ellen couldn't bring herself to call Cecily's mother. Mrs. Vandering had make it clear yesterday that she felt Ellen's legitimate interest in the child was at an end. But would Cecily's father feel that way? She turned back to the phone book.

Howard Vandering's residence wasn't listed. But there was a number for Vandering Enterprises on Madison Avenue. She dialed, spoke to a switchboard operator, a secretary, and still another secretary.

"Please hold on, Miss Stacey. I'll see if Mr. Vandering is in."

Within seconds a man's voice said, "Miss Stacey, this is Howard Vandering." He sounded both eager and cautious. "Are you the young lady who was up at the Cloisters yesterday?"

She said, equally mindful of the switchboard operator, "Yes, I'm the one."

"Would it be possible for you to come to my office?"

"Right now?"

"If it's convenient."

"All right. I'm only a few blocks away."

"Please don't bother stopping at the reception desk on the sixteenth floor. Come straight to my office on the eighteenth."

As a secretary ushered her ten minutes later into a wood-paneled office, a dark-haired man, tall and heavy-set and apparently in his late forties, advanced to meet her. His smile didn't alter the look of chronic anxiety in his dark eyes.

"This is kind of you, Miss Stacey. I'm Howard Vandering." As they shook hands, Ellen noticed that a second man, thin and blond, had got up from one of the red leather chairs facing a massive desk.

Howard Vandering said, "This is my brother Leonard, Miss Stacey."

Exchanging smiles with the blond man, Ellen felt surprise. He looked at least fifteen years younger than Howard Vandering. Perhaps her reaction showed, because Howard Vandering said, "Len and I are half-brothers." He moved behind his desk. "Please sit down, Miss Stacey."

When they were all seated, Howard Vandering said, "First of all, I'd like to thank you for bringing my daughter home."

She murmured an acknowledgment.

"Would you like to tell me about it, Miss Stacey? Speak freely. I have no secrets from Len."

"There's not much to tell. I found her on the terrace at the Cloisters, phoned her mother, and brought her home."

"Did she say anything?"

"Yes, but your—but Mrs. Vandering dismissed it as nonsense, and I suppose it was. Cecily told me she hadn't bought the drug. Someone had given it to her. I think her exact words were, 'I don't have to buy. They give it to me.' "

"They?" Howard's brother asked.

She looked at the younger man, confirming her first impression that he was attractive. Eyes as gray as his young niece's. Firm, pleasant features. "She didn't tell me who they were, and I didn't ask. For one thing, I doubted that I'd get a coherent answer. For another, I felt I had no right to question her extensively, since I was neither her parent nor her doctor."

"Well, I doubt that any of us will get anyplace." Howard Vandering's voice was heavy. "I called Dr. Carson at his clinic about an hour ago, and he told me he hadn't even tried to question her yet. Anyway, I don't suppose any of us will get any farther than we did the last—"

He broke off. Ellen said, with embarrassment, "Mrs. Vandering told me there had been a similar episode last spring."

"I see."

There was a brief silence. Then Howard Vandering asked, "Did my daughter say anything else?"

"Yes, on the way home in the cab. Apparently she thought for a moment that I was someone named Amy."

She stopped speaking, arrested by the leap of pain in Howard Vandering's eyes. After a moment he said, "Amy Thornhill was someone very dear to me, and to my daughter. Please go on, Miss Stacey."

Ellen said reluctantly, "When she realized I wasn't this other person, she said, 'You'd better stay away from me, or they'll get you the way they got Amy.' I asked her who Amy was, and she said something like, 'She was my friend, and so they killed her.'"

Cecily's father said, "Oh, my God!" Then, after a moment: "Amy was killed by robbers who broke into her apartment. Her befriending Cecily had nothing to do with it. If Cecily had talked to me about it, I could have told her so. But she said nothing. And so she's gone around

47

tormenting herself with some grotesque idea—"

He broke off. Ellen said, "It's often like that. Parents are the last people some children confide in."

He sent her a grateful look. It was good to be reminded that other parents felt shut out, helpless to reach a child desperately in need of help.

Ellen asked hesitantly, "May I phone you in a few days to ask how Cecily is?"

"Of course. What's more, I'd like it very much if you would see her again."

"See her? Why?"

"She remembers you. Dr. Carson told me that she said of you, 'I liked her. She was nice.' "

The twist of bittersweet emotion she felt, Ellen knew, was both for the living child and the one who had looked back over Richard's shoulder.

"I don't know," she said. After all, it might be unwise to draw close to the child. Probably she couldn't help Cecily. Probably all she would do would be to make herself unhappy over the child's unhappiness. "I'll see," she said finally.

"Well, I guess that's all I could expect. Again, I'm very grateful to you."

As she rose, the two men also got to their feet. She shook hands with Howard Vandering, and then turned to the younger man.

"I'm leaving too," he said, grinding out his cigarette in an onyx tray on his brother's desk. "See you, Howard."

Out in the hall Leonard Vandering pressed the elevator button and then asked, without preamble, "Will you have dinner with me tonight?"

She answered, startled, "Is there something about your

niece you would like to talk over with me?"

"That would make a good excuse. But the truth is, I'd like to know you better."

She looked at him doubtfully. Attractive, yes. But if, like Charles . . .

"I'm not," he said. "I've never been."

"Never been?"

"Married."

She laughed.

"Seven o'clock all right with you?"

"Yes," she said, and gave him her address.

Over broiled swordfish in an eastside restaurant, Ellen told him, in response to his questions, a little about her work as an actress. Then she said, "How about you? Are you part of Vandering Enterprises?"

"No, that's entirely Howard's baby. That, and the Vandering money. My father left me twenty thousand dollars and his blessing."

Disconcerted by his cheerful frankness, Ellen searched for a suitable answer. Finally she said, "That seems odd."

"It wasn't really. Howard was always the heavy favorite with Dad. Besides, he didn't like the way I blew the money I inherited from my mother's sister when I was twenty."

Ellen smiled. "Wine, women, and song?"

"Some went for that. Most of it I spent on three schooners for inter-island trade in the Caribbean. Dad pointed out that I knew as much about the shipping business as I knew about quantum physics, and he was right. I went broke within a year."

"It does seem a rather odd business to have gone into."

"Not for a kid who was hung up on Joseph Conrad."

49

"What do you do now?"

"Paint. Sculpt a little."

Something in his tone made her say, "Should I have heard of you? If so, I'm sorry. About the only contemporary painter I could name offhand is Andrew Wyeth."

He laughed. "I'm not in his class. But the pictures I do now are representational, like his. I reversed the usual progression. Started out abstract, and ended up where I am now." He paused. "I'd like for you to see some of my work."

"I'd like to."

"We could go to my place after dinner. I have an apartment and a studio in a loft on the lower eastside."

She gave him a long, considering look.

Again he laughed. "I'm asking you to see my work. Anything else that might happen would be strictly up to you."

An hour later, climbing worn stairs where garbage cans stood outside scarred doors on the landings, she felt a pronounced uneasiness. True, the man climbing slightly ahead of her up the third flight belonged to one of America's most well-known families. True, his manner was open and pleasant. But this neighborhood! Too, his former sister-in-law obviously disapproved of him, and perhaps for more reason than the marijuana his niece had found in his apartment.

As they approached the next landing, a door opened, and a girl of about twenty, in a tie-dyed garment that looked like a man's elongated undershirt, peered out at them. Her feet were bare. So was the solemn-faced baby she carried on her left hip.

"Hi, Len. I thought you were someone else."

"Hi, Barbara. What do you hear from Charlie?"

"Oh, he's fine. He works in the prison library now." She smiled at both of them and closed the door.

"Her husband swung on two members of his draft board," Len said. "Well, one more flight."

The door on the next landing bore a padlock. "Junkies," he explained, fishing in a pocket for the key. "If you let them, they'll steal you blind."

"Do you *like* living down here?"

"Sure. Except for the junkies, everybody's great. Not just the kids. The old people who've been here since Cleveland was president are nice, too. Why, right next door there's this old poet, the only man in America publishing poetry written in Yiddish."

He had the door open by then. Reaching inside, he switched on the light.

Ellen stepped across the threshold and looked around her. Walls paneled in satiny dark wood. A lowered ceiling, holding recessed lights that shed a soft glow over expensive brown carpeting, and chairs and sofas of modern design, and a low table, no doubt made to order, of massive planks six inches thick.

"Like it?"

"I think it's beautiful." She also thought it incomprehensible. Why choose a neighborhood filled with junkies, hippies, and people too poor or too old to move elsewhere, and then spend many thousands on your apartment?

He seemed to read her thoughts. "As I said, I like the people down here. But since I can afford to live differently than they do, why shouldn't I?"

He moved across the room to a hi-fi set, touched a switch. Kurt Weil's overture to *The Three Penny Opera*, tinnily melodious and yet wry, poured into the room. "How about taking a drink with us on the gallery tour? Scotch and water all right? I think that's all I've got."

51

"Fine."

Through the doorway of the pullman kitchen, she watched him uncork a bottle and take ice from the refrigerator. When he had returned to the living room and handed her a glass, he said, "This way."

On the opposite side of the room he reached inside an open doorway and switched on fluorescent tubes, hung beneath the skylighted roof. Stepping past him into the studio, Ellen looked at unframed canvases hung along one wall, and a rough table littered with paint-stained rags and brushes set in jars. Then she cried, "What's *that?*"

In one corner stood four life-sized figures in street clothing—two adult men and a woman and a small boy—apparently molded out of plaster. Eyes and lips had been colored, but otherwise the figures were of unrelieved whiteness. The right hand of the older man rested on the other man's shoulder. All four figures stared straight ahead with bright, identical smiles.

"That's from my pop art period. I called it 'Family Group.' Dad, Mother, Big Brother, and Little Brother."

Drawing close to the figures, Ellen said, puzzled, "But they seem to be wearing masks."

"Not seem to. Are. That's the whole point."

One by one he disengaged the white elastic bands which, running behind the plaster heads, held the masks in place, and laid them on the littered table. "There."

Ellen felt shock. All the figures, except the little boy's, still smiled, but the quality of their smiles had altered. Now the father, looking sidewise, smiled with paternal pride at his elder son, whose own smile looked a bit vacuous. The woman's smile, directed at the viewer, had such a strained, anxious quality that it was almost a grimace of pain. And

52

the little boy's face, as he directed his gaze upward at his father and brother, held an envious longing tinged with unchildlike bitterness.

Ellen cried involuntarily, "Why did you do it?"

"To get it out of my system. It was cheaper, quicker, and less painful than psychoanalysis."

"Was your family really like that?"

"Pretty much so. Of course when I was six years old, I didn't understand why. It was only over the years that I pieced the whole thing together. Howard's mother, I gradually learned, had been one of those retiring types interested in nothing but her family. That must have been rough on Dad, because he loved parties and people. He was the only man I've ever known who actually enjoyed those big charity balls. And so, after his first wife died, he married a frivolous extrovert."

"She doesn't look frivolous."

"That was my fault, or so Dad must have felt. After I was born, she underwent one of those complete transformations, like Becket after King Henry was foolish enough to make him Archbishop. She changed into one of those anxious, child-centered women, ninety-nine percent mother and one percent wife."

He paused, and then went on, "I can see why he never cottoned to me. In a sense, I'd deprived him of her. Once I'd understood that, I got over that particular hangup."

Ellen thought, "Did you?" Could anyone ever recover fully from the pain and jealousy depicted in that small figure's face?

Taking her arm, he led her toward the three paintings hung on the wall. "Maybe you'll like my pictures better."

She liked them much better. The first canvas showed

an old man in a yarmulke, seated at a paper-strewn table. Wintry gray light coming through a window silhouetted his lean, beautiful profile. She guessed, "America's only Yiddish poet?"

"That's right."

When she looked at the next picture, she burst out laughing. Painted in the stiff style of Grant Wood's American Gothic, a hippie couple stared grimly back at her. The girl, lank-haired and with an Indian headband tied across her forehead, was undoubtedly his downstairs neighbor, Barbara. Her bearded companion held, in place of Grant Wood's pitchfork, a peace symbol affixed to a wooden shaft.

"The draft board assaulter?"

"Yes, that's Charlie. I finished the picture two days before he lost his appeal. What do you think of this last one?"

It was a portrait of Cecily Vandering, curly dark head tilted against a red velvet chair back. The pointed-chinned face didn't smile. The gray eyes, although looking directly at the viewer, seemed to be gazing inward.

"It's good," Ellen said slowly. "Has Mrs. Vandering seen it?"

"She doesn't even know of its existence. I painted it during weekends last winter when Cecily stayed with Howard." He paused. "Janet wouldn't like it."

"No." Of course she wouldn't. No mother would like to see her child's sad, inexplicable alienation depicted in a painting.

They moved back into the living room. As he started to sit down beside her on one of the low sofas, he looked at her glass and said, "Hey, your drink needs freshening."

"Please don't. I'll finish this, and then I'd better go. I have a lot of things to do around the apartment tomorrow, and tomorrow night I have a movie job."

He said, sitting down beside her, "What sort of part is it?"

She laughed. "You could scarcely call it a part. I'm to wear a long white dress. I'll have no lines, and the set is an old abandoned movie theater on upper Broadway."

He frowned. "You mean you'll be just an extra? What about status? After all, if you've starred in summer stock—"

"Theater people no longer worry much about status. Even big stars do commercials. As for actresses like me, we take about anything we can get."

"I see." He rattled the ice in his glass. "Not to change the subject—why do people always say that before they change the subject?—but anyway, what about Cecily? Do you intend to see her again, as Howard suggested?"

"I don't know," Ellen said slowly. "You're her uncle. Do you think it would be a good idea?"

"Good for her, perhaps. And Lord knows the poor kid needs any help she can get. But I don't know whether it would be good for you. And after all, she's not your child."

Ellen said lightly, "You mean that perhaps I'd better mind my own business?"

"I'd never put it that way."

"I'm sure you wouldn't. I was just reminded of an anonymous phone call I received last night."

"An obscene call?"

"No. This man—I'm almost certain it was a man—told me that if I wanted to stay healthy, I'd better mind my own business. Then he hung up."

"That was all he said? Just mind your own business?"

"That was all."

He laughed. "Sounds to me as if someone has hit upon another line that can be used against anybody. You know, like, 'Leave town. All is discovered.' "

When she looked at him questioningly, he added, "You don't know the story? That was the telegram some practical joker sent to twenty of the most prominent men in his community. Nineteen of them left town the next day."

She smiled. "I see what you mean. Almost everyone has something to hide. And most people—everyone who gossips, for instance—are mixed up in things that aren't strictly their own business."

"That's it."

"Then you think he's made that same call to lots of women?"

"Of course."

"I think so too. But you see, the call came only a few hours after I'd brought Cecily home from the Cloisters. And so it did cross my mind that the two things might be connected."

He stared at her, apparently puzzled. "How could they be? True, Janet's so afraid of publicity that she might try to discourage any outsider's interest in Cecily. But I can't imagine her making such a phone call, or arranging for anyone else to do so. And all the others close to Cecily would be glad of her getting help from anyone."

Ellen nodded. No point in mentioning again Cecily's reference to "they." All of those surrounding the child—her parents, her young uncle, and probably even her doctor—seemed to think those shadowy figures were either fantasy or Cecily's attempt to throw dust in adult eyes.

He said, "Then you haven't decided whether or not you'll see Cecily again?"

"No, I haven't decided. Len, this has been lovely, but I really must go home now."

She started to rise. Grasping her wrist, he drew her down beside him and kissed her lightly. "Do you really have to go?"

"I have to. Tomorrow's a busy day."

He sighed and got to his feet. "All right, I'll telephone for a cab. In this neighborhood we'd have to walk blocks before we found one."

six

At eight the next evening, flanked by two of her colleagues
—a gray-haired English-born actress and a plump young
woman who often played children's roles in radio commercials—Ellen moved along a dimly lit passageway behind the old movie theater's first balcony. Ahead of them,
showing the way, walked a young assistant director named
Gene Walsh. The air smelled of dust and old carpeting and
mice. From somewhere up ahead in the dimness came the
rasp of a hacksaw cutting through steel, and the agonized
shriek of a nail withdrawn from wood.

"My God," Araminta Lee said in her fluty English voice,
"are they tearing the place down over our heads?"

"Yeah," Gene answered, as two workmen, one carrying
a toolbox and the other an acetylene torch, hurried past
them. "Guess the wreckers are behind in their contract.
Watch out for those rails there."

Ellen maneuvered past two stacks of steel rails and then
looked to her right, through the arched entrance of a
balcony aisle. On the distant stage, under the shouted orders of a tall young director in a baseball cap, a crew was
rigging booms and rolling arc lamps into place.

"Well," Gene said, "here's where you change, girls."

He had stopped beside a door. On it, affixed at the top edge by Scotch tape, a piece of yellow paper bore the words, printed in pencil, "Ladies' Dressing Room."

With a suspicious flare of her high-cut nostrils, Araminta Lee stepped forward, lifted the paper by its lower edge, and then whirled on the assistant director. "You're putting us in the men's room!"

"Now look—"

"One no longer expects star treatment," the actress who had once shared a stage with Olivier swept on bitterly, "but one would think you would at least put us in the ladies' room."

"Can't. They're tearing out the fixtures in there. It's all right," he wheedled. "You'll be just in the front part, and we fixed it up nice—chairs, a mirror, everything." He pushed the door open. "See?"

Over Araminta's shoulder, Ellen looked into the little anteroom. Three straight chairs stood on the tiled floor. Against one wall was a battered dressing table, with a mirror hanging above it. Beside the mirror, three wire hangers dangled from a nail. "Make it as fast as you can, girls," Gene said, and hurried away.

They carried their suitcases inside and set them down. "Girls!" Araminta said. "Why, I could be that pup's grandmother." She stared at the closed and bolted double doors to the inner sanctum. "What keeps one in the acting profession is the sheer glamor of it."

"Oh, yes!" Jane Bartlett agreed, in the six-year-old voice she used to extol peanut butter, breakfast foods, and toys, "that's what makes it so super!"

Ellen smiled. Actresses. They were always complaining

and always coming back for more. "He said make it fast," she reminded them, and knelt to open her suitcase.

A few minutes later, each garbed in pristine white, they sat and looked at each other. "I wonder if we're supposed to be brides," Jane said.

"Debutantes," Araminta corrected, and grunted slightly as she bent to take a knitting bag from her suitcase.

"Three missing links," Ellen said, "from a Vassar daisy chain."

For perhaps a minute, the only sound was the click of knitting needles. Then there was a knock at the door. "Okay, girls. On the set."

They emerged into the dim passageway. "This is just a rehearsal," Gene said. "Ellen, you'll stand at the top of the center aisle. Araminta will be at the top of the right, and Jane at the left. When I give the signal, you're to run down the aisles to the balcony railing, lean out over it, look down, and scream."

"Run?" Araminta said. "At my time of life?"

"It's downhill," he pointed out, "and it's a ramp, not steps, and you can take your shoes off."

"Very well, but if I break any bones, I'll sue the bloody lot of you."

"Sure, sure. Okay, places."

Moving to the head of the center aisle, Ellen looked down the ramp to the low wall at the balcony's edge, surmounted by a waist-high railing. Beyond it and far below, the director stood holding a hand mike. Except for two gaffers stationed behind arc lamps, the crew had left the stage.

"Ready up there, Gene?" His amplified voice echoed hollowly in the almost empty theater.

Seated in an aisle seat two-thirds of the way toward the

front of the balcony, Gene called back, "We're ready, Mr. Claypool."

"All right, ladies. We'll see how it's going to look. Now when you hit the railing, give me a good loud scream. Okay, lights."

The arc lamps came on, so dazzling that Ellen knew she wouldn't have been able to see the stage even if she had been looking toward it, rather than at Gene. Turned sidewise in the aisle seat, he made a beckoning gesture with both hands.

Ellen ran down the long slope. Dazzled by the lights, she fetched up against the rail sooner than she had expected to, and with a force that knocked the wind out of her. Nevertheless, as she leaned out and looked down at the rows of chair backs below, she found she had enough breath to scream.

"That's fine," the director called, "except for one thing. Will the lady in the center aisle scream a little louder next time?"

The lights went out. Momentarily blinded, Ellen called, "I'll try."

"Fine. Return to your dressing room, ladies. We'll be set for the take in fifteen minutes."

Hands groping from the back of one aisle seat to another, Ellen climbed the ramp to the corridor and, with some of her vision returning, went into the dressing room and sat down on a chair. A moment later she was joined by Araminta and Jane.

"I wonder," Ellen said, "if the Screen Actors' Guild would back me up in a compensation claim for a bruised stomach."

"You too?" Jane said.

"Keep your hands in front of you next time," Araminta

advised. "That's what I did." She reached down for her knitting.

After a moment Jane said, "I wonder what this picture is about."

"Maybe it's a remake," Ellen said, "only this time they're going to call it *Phantoms of the Opera.*"

Chuckling, Araminta began to knit. For a while there was no sound except that of the steel needles. Then the door opened. A man in blue denim shirt and trousers, with a construction worker's yellow helmet on his head, stared at the white-gowned women, one of them serenely knitting. The bewildered astonishment on his face gave way to horror. Backing away, he let the door swing closed.

For several seconds there was silence. Then, rising, Araminta said in a thoughtful tone, "Now I wonder—"

She went out into the corridor, returning almost immediately. "I was right. That piece of paper fell down."

Ellen asked, "Did you put it back up?"

"Of course not. If they keep us waiting much longer, maybe we'll be able to shock the bejeezus out of another one."

But she was doomed to disappointment. Less than a minute later, Gene knocked and said, "We're ready for the take, girls."

Again Ellen stood at the top of the aisle. The arc lamps came on, blindingly. She kept her gaze fixed on Gene, dimly visible in his aisle seat. A clapboard sounded, and she knew the cameras were turning. Gene beckoned.

She ran, this time with arms bent and hands held at waist height, toward the blinding glare. Her hands touched the metal rail, gripped it. She leaned out over it.

And then she screamed, but the scream was genuine, because the section of rail had given way from its stanchion at one end, tearing itself from the grasp of her left hand. As the rail swung out over the dazzling void, her right hand remained frozen to the metal, pulling her overbalanced body along with it. As if time had stretched itself into ghastly slow motion, a second seemed minutes—minutes in which she hung there, aware of her thighs being drawn across the top of the low balcony wall. Then she managed to loosen the deadly grip of her right hand. With a desperate twist of her body, she flung an arm backward. The fingers of her right hand found the stanchion, circled it, tried to hang on. But her own weight was pulling her fingers loose. She heard shouts, and then a metallic clang as the rail, falling free of its other stanchion, struck the sharp edges of the seat back below. . . .

A hand caught her right wrist. An arm hooked itself around her waist. Still with that sense of time passing with infinite slowness, she felt herself pulled back onto the balcony, felt her feet touch the ramp.

Gene asked shakily, his arm still around her, "You all right?"

She managed to move her lips. "Yes."

From below, Mr. Claypool's amplified voice called, "Is she hurt?"

"I don't think so," Gene shouted back.

"Somebody get lights on in the balcony. And kill these lights down here."

Kill. She had almost been . . .

She slumped against Gene's chest. Before he lowered her into an aisle seat, she was aware of two white-clad figures moving swiftly down the ramp toward her.

seven

Around eleven the next morning, still clad in a nightgown and robe, Ellen sat in an armchair drawn up to her open front window. Apparently this was to be one of those years of no spring. Last Monday, New Yorkers had shivered in temperatures only a little above freezing. Now the sunlight pouring through the screen was as warm as July's. Overnight the leaves of the plane tree across the street had taken on a deep summer green.

She felt a slight cloudiness of mind and heaviness of body. That, she knew, was due to the pills she had taken the night before. At Mr. Claypool's insistence, she had gone in a taxi with Gene and Araminta Lee to a hospital. There a doctor had checked her over and given her one sleeping capsule and three small white pills which, he explained, would relax her muscular stiffness. When she protested that she didn't feel stiff, he said, "You will."

He'd been right. When she awakened that morning, just getting out of bed had been a painful effort. But now, what with the hot shower she had taken and the summery sunlight pouring through the window, she felt almost normal except for one thing—the puzzled thoughts awakened in her by a phone call from Gene Walsh.

He had phoned only minutes ago. When she tried to thank him again, he had said, "What was I supposed to do? Let you drop? What I'm calling about is that rail that gave way. Mr. Claypool and the company's insurance man went prowling around the theater until all hours last night, and again this morning."

"And?" Her stomach tightened with the memory of hanging in space, hand frozen to that rail.

"Near as anybody can figure out, here's what happened. Before Mr. Claypool decided to rent the place for forty-eight hours, the wrecking company had taken down the railings from both balconies. He hired his own crew to put back the railings and rehang some chandeliers, and so on. One of the workmen must have made a mistake. The rail section that gave way belonged to the upper balcony, where the sections are a fraction of an inch shorter than those in the first balcony. It was long enough to remain in place, but not long enough to screw solidly into the stachions on each side of it."

Ellen frowned. "But it felt so solid when I ran into it during rehearsal. It almost knocked the breath out of me."

"I know. You mentioned that in the taxi. All they can figure out is that you jarred it almost loose the first time, and so the second time—"

He broke off, and then added, "By the way, I think the company's insurance man is going to offer you a hundred bucks as settlement."

His carefully neutral tone told her that he considered it far too little. So did she. But she would accept it. Actresses of minor stature who became branded as "troublesome" soon found themselves scanning the sales positions ads.

"Thanks for telling me. Oh, one other thing. What's that picture about?"

"Search me. All I do is yell, 'On the set!' But I do know the working title. It's *Farewell, Sweet Pistachio.*"

Ellen laughed.

"Well, I'd better get back on the job. See you around, I hope."

When she had hung up, Ellen's face still wore an amused smile. But as she moved back to her chair beside the window, her smile had faded. It seemed strange indeed that the rail, after withstanding the first jolting impact of her body, should give way under much less force twenty minutes later.

Now a sudden thought made her stiffen. What if it hadn't been the same rail? What if someone, during those twenty minutes, had removed the rail and put a shorter one in its place?

She sat very still, eyes fixed unseeingly on a second-floor window box, bright with King Alfred daffodils and Red Emperor tulips, across the street.

At least thirty men in workclothes—the wreckers, and the film company's grips and gaffers and camera crew—had been moving about that old movie house the night before. One or even two men who had no legitimate business there could have mingled with them unchallenged, their only disguise rolled-up shirt sleeves and a wrench or hammer carried in one hand. And the substitution would have been a simple matter. Those two stacks of rails—undoubtedly sorted into those for the upper and lower balconies—had lain in the corridor for anyone to pick up. Two minutes' work with a wrench there in the balcony's near darkness, and another rail, shorter by a small but deadly fraction of an inch, could have been installed.

But why? Why should anyone have tried to send an obscure actress plunging to her death?

The child, with her mumbled words about "they." That warning phone call Monday night.

Now stop it, she told herself. No one connected with Cecily Vandering even knew she was going to be in that old movie house.

Then she realized she was wrong about that. Leonard Vandering had known. She had told him that she would be working Wednesday night in an abandoned movie theater on upper Broadway. He could easily have learned which theater. For one thing, the film company's truck must have been parked outside for several hours before she reported to the set.

No! Despite that disturbing "Family Group," she liked Len. She couldn't imagine him moving about that old theater in workmen's guise, or hiring anyone to do so.

Could it have been someone else?

It could have been almost anyone, she realized now, and especially anyone who knew she sometimes worked in films. Even people who had never watched a picture being made knew that the confusion of a movie set—actors and technicians milling about, brilliantly lighted areas contrasting with shadowy ones, overhead equipment that might fall, and camera cables that might trip one up—offered an ideal place for staging an accident.

Suppose someone had set himself to watch her movements. She could imagine him following her as, suitcase in hand, she traveled on the Lexington Avenue subway to Ninety-sixth Street, and then on the crosstown bus to Broadway. Once inside the theater he could have shed his coat, picked up a tool, and then wandered about making up his mind what sort of accident was to occur. She thought of him watching from one of those old-fashioned boxes as, during the rehearsal, she ran down the ramp to collide with that rail.

She tried for a moment to recall the faces of individual workmen she had seen moving about last night. Except in one case, it was no use. The exception was the man who had innocently opened the door of what he assumed to be the men's room, and it was impossible to think of his stupefied face, round and guileless under his hard hat, as that of a murderer.

And anyway, she told herself, her thoughts coming full circle, it was absurd to keep mulling over the possibility that it hadn't been an accident. Every day people suffered injuries, and even death, because of someone's careless workmanship—a subway train with improperly aligned brakes, a baby's crib mistakenly painted with poisonous, lead-based paint, an automobile passing off the assembly line with some small but death-dealing flaw.

Even so, did she have the right to dismiss completely last night's incident? On her own behalf, yes. But what about Cecily Vandering? If there was even the remotest chance that the child was the victim of some malevolent person, someone who wanted to keep her lonely, friendless, confiding in no one . . .

There was only one thing to do. See the child's father again. Remind him of the things his daughter had said to her, and tell him about the anonymous phone call and her own near-fatal accident. Then she would leave the matter in his hands, to be dismissed or investigated as he chose.

She was already moving toward the phone when it rang. "Ellen? This is Len Vandering."

68

Her nerves tightened. "Oh, hello. How are you?"

"Couldn't be better. And you?"

After a moment she said deliberately. "I'm fairly well, considering that I almost got killed last night."

"You *what?*"

"A balcony rail gave way in the old movie house I told you about. It crashed into the orchestra seats, and I nearly went with it."

"My God." He paused. "But you're all right?"

"Except for the jitters and a slightly wrenched back."

"You ought to sue the pants off that movie company. If they were the ones at fault, I mean."

"They were," she said dryly, "but I won't sue. I'd rather go on getting movie jobs."

"Like that, huh?" he said, after a moment. "Seems a damned shame. Want to have dinner tonight and tell me more about it?"

"I'm sorry, but I don't feel up to going out." Attractive as she found Leonard Vandering, it might be wise to have that talk with his brother before she saw any more of him.

"Tomorrow night, then?"

It could be days before she talked to Howard Vandering. "I'm afraid I'll be busy the rest of this week."

His voice stiffened slightly. "Shall I call you the first of next week?"

"Please do."

"Fine. And I hope to see you then."

She looked up Vandering Enterprises in the phone book, dialed. As before, she was switched to a secretary and then to Howard Vandering's personal secretary. "This is Ellen Stacey. May I speak to Mr. Vandering?"

"I'm sorry, but Mr. Vandering is in Toledo."

69

"Could you tell me when he'll be back?"

"I can't say for sure. Perhaps Mr. Reardon could. Suppose I have this call switched to him."

"Mr. Reardon?"

"Mr. Daniel Reardon, Mr. Vandering's partner. Wait just a moment."

Ellen spoke briefly with another secretary. Then a deep voice said, "Hello there, Miss Stacey." Ellen's stage-trained ear caught the accent of the borough across the river. "I'm Dan Reardon."

"Hello, Mr. Reardon. Could you tell me when Mr. Vandering will be back?"

"Not until the weekend. Anything I can do for you? I mean, is it something about his daughter?"

"Why, how did you—"

"Howard and I are pretty close, Miss Stacey. He told me all about the business at the Cloisters Monday, and about your visit to his office Tuesday." He paused. "You want his phone number in Toledo? If it's important, he'll want to fly back."

It would be hard to give Howard Vandering over the phone an explanation of her uneasiness. And she didn't want to risk bringing him back with a few vague but alarming phrases, especially since he might well decide, after he got here, that her anxiety had been groundless.

"Miss Stacey? You still there?"

"Yes."

"Maybe you'd rather talk to me about it. Then I could advise you as to whether or not you should call Toledo." When she didn't answer, he said, "Of course, if it's too personal—"

"I don't think it is. If he discusses his daughter's—dif-

70

ficulties with you, I don't think he would mind my talking to you about this matter."

"Then how about meeting me for lunch?"

"Today? It's so late." She glanced at her watch. Twenty of twelve.

"Could you make it by one-thirty?"

"Easily."

He named an expensive and famous restaurant in the east Sixties. "I'll get there a little early. Just tell the maitre d' you're having lunch with me."

eight

It was a measure of Dan Reardon's importance, Ellen realized, that the maitre d' himself led her through the maze of well-dressed people seated at white-clothed tables, each with its crystal vase of cut flowers. At a leather-upholstered banquette against one wall, her host had got to his feet. She saw a handsome man in his middle thirties, with curly dark hair, tanned, engagingly tough features, and dark blue eyes which at the moment looked both pleased and surprised.

When they were seated, he said, "Howard told me you were an actress. You look more like a schoolteacher."

"Oh, please!"

"I meant it as a compliment. Some of the best-looking girls around are teachers, these days. I meant that you look—well, nice."

"Thank you." Feeling amused and flattered, she saw that he seemed disconcerted, even a little shy. And that, surely, was something rare for Dan Reardon. To judge by a squib she had once read about him in *Time,* he was ordinarily about as shy as an embattled rhino.

When a waiter had taken their order for Manhattans,

Dan Reardon asked, "You want to tell me right now what's on your mind, or do you want to wait?"

"I'd rather tell you now," she said, and then fell silent, not knowing how to begin.

"You said it was about Cecily," he prompted.

"Yes. Has her father told you the things she said to me?"

"You mean that stuff about someone giving her dope, and someone killing Amy Thornhill because she was the kid's friend? He told me."

"Well, the things she said struck me as fantastic, of course. Her parents feel the same way, and I suppose you do, too. But Monday night—"

The waiter was beside them, carrying their drinks on a tray, and with a menu card tucked under his arm. He took their orders for veal Marengo, and disappeared.

Ellen went on, telling of the anonymous phone call she had received. "And two nights later, I reported for this movie job."

With Dan Reardon's gaze never leaving her face, she described the terror of the moment when she was sure she was about to plunge through the blinding light to the theater orchestra. It seemed to her that by the time she had finished, his face had paled a little beneath its tan.

She said, "This morning I added it up. The things Cecily said, the phone call, and then the balcony rail. Now please don't misunderstand. I realize there's little chance these things have anything to do with each other. You read of much stranger coincidences in the newspapers."

He nodded. "I know. A Mary Jones driving east on Jones Street crashes into a John Jones, no relation, and is haled into court before Judge William Jones. But all the same—"

"All the same, I thought I ought to tell Mr. Vandering.

Maybe he'll feel that it would be wiser to have Cecily guarded by a detective from now on."

He frowned. "I suggested that over a year ago, the first time they found out she had been sniffing heroin. Mrs. Vandering turned thumbs down. She said it would have a bad effect on Cecily. My hunch is she knew the kid's school wouldn't stand for it. If word got out that some flatfoot was hanging around to keep one of the little girls from getting her hands on dope, the school might wind up with a lot of empty desks."

The Mainwaring School. Amanda Mainwaring, with her straight, aristocratic figure, her fine-featured old face, and the faded eyes that had grown suddenly bright and bitter.

Dan Reardon asked, "What is it?"

"Something I'd forgotten until now. After I left Mrs. Vandering's apartment last Monday, I walked past Cecily's school. An old lady who said her name was Amanda Mainwaring stopped and talked to me. Do you know anything about her?"

"I know her stockbroker. He told me about her house in the east Sixties. It's filled with antiques, and he tried to buy some, but no dice."

"She owns an entire house?"

"Yes. She inherited the house and a bundle of money twenty years ago."

Not just a slightly mad old lady, then. An old lady who had money, perhaps enough to hire almost any sort of service she might require—

"But to get back to the kid," Dan Reardon said. "I'll tell Howard again that there ought to be a detective watching her. Maybe this time he'll be able to convince her mother." He paused. "But how about you?"

She smiled. "I can't afford a private detective. And I doubt that I could make the police believe I needed a bodyguard, especially when I don't believe it myself. I've decided to dismiss the whole thing."

After a moment he said very quietly, "All right, but I hope you'll look both ways before crossing a street from now on."

"And keep my door locked and bolted. I intend to."

"Now how about another drink?"

"No, thank you."

"Then I won't have one either. Besides, here comes our lunch."

When the waiter had left, Ellen asked, "Do you know Leonard Vandering?"

"Howard's kid brother? Sure. Why do you ask?"

"I had dinner with him last Tuesday night." She hesitated, and then asked, "What do you think of him?"

"Oh, he's all right, I guess. But he's sort of a kook. Why live in a slum if you don't have to? Me, I was raised in a cold-water flat with the bathtub in the kitchen. Now that I can afford it, I intend to go strictly first class the rest of my life."

"The cold-water flat was in Brooklyn?"

He nodded. "On a solidly Italian block in Red Hook."

"But aren't you Irish?"

"Only half. My mother was Italian. When I was a year old, my old man skipped out. We never heard from him again. Then when I was three, my mother died, so I went to live with her parents."

"That—that sounds awful."

"Oh, it wasn't so bad. My grandparents were a nice old couple. And sure it was a poor neighborhood, and a tough

75

one, but at least in those days you didn't have to nail your door up at night to keep the junkies out."

A sweetly reproachful voice said, "Why, Danny! Long time no see."

Ellen looked up. The girl standing beside the table was tall and brunette and beautiful. Her brown eyes rested with cool appraisal on Ellen's face for a moment, and then returned to Dan Reardon.

He remained seated. "Hello, Delphine. How've you been?"

"Fine. Danny, have you opened your place in the Hamptons yet?"

"I opened it last month."

"And you haven't asked me out there!"

"I will, honey, real soon."

"Don't forget." Again she gave Ellen an appraising, faintly hostile look. " 'By now," she said, and walked away.

Ellen said, looking after her, "She's beautiful."

"Yes, she's a good-looking girl. I didn't introduce you because—well, let's put it this way. Delphine isn't the kind of girl you take home to meet Mother."

Whereas she, Ellen, presumably was. Again she felt amused. What an odd mixture he was. Brash, and probably even ruthless. She was sure that an ex-Red Hook boy couldn't climb to almost the top of the financial heap without bashing in a few ribs. And yet there had been that flattering look of pleased surprise when she approached his table. And now this display of old-fashioned discrimination between "nice" women and the other kind.

She said, "Do you know many beautiful girls?"

"Like Delphine, you mean? Sure. It's expected of me. If you've fought your way up in this town, and especially if you're a bachelor, you're supposed to be seen around with beautiful women. That's all they are for me, though. Window dressing. Now why the smile?"

"Because I think you're a liar."

He laughed. "Sure. I'm a liar and a scoundrel. Just ask anybody."

"So you have a house out in the Hamptons."

"Who doesn't?"

"I haven't, for instance."

"Well, maybe sometime you'll—"

He broke off, and she realized, again with amusement, that he had been about to invite her for the weekend.

"What I mean is," he said, "that nearly everyone I know has a house out there. My place isn't far from Len Vandering's house in one direction, and Howard's in the other. Only I think it's all Mrs. Vandering's now. Part of the divorce settlement, I guess."

"Sounds cozy, like the compound at Hyannisport."

"Not exactly. I don't even see Len or Mrs. Vandering except when I run into them at some really big cocktail party. Those parties! All some people do out there is break out the booze for each other. Sometimes I wonder why they don't get Raffles or some club like that to install sun lamps and a big swimming pool near the bar. Then they could stay right in the city all summer."

"Well, to judge by that tan, you don't spend your weekends drinking indoors."

"Oh, that's from the sun lamps at the Midtown Club. Come to think of it, the first time I talked to Howard was under those lamps."

She waited until a bus boy had removed their plates, and then asked, "Do you enjoy being Mr. Vandering's partner?"

"Sure. I'm a tinkerer. I like to take a bunch of companies some other guy hasn't done too well with, and sell some, and expand others, and switch executives from one spot to another. It's a hell of a lot more fun than playing the market, which was how I started out."

"I once knew an actress who had made quite a lot of money in the stock market. She told me I ought to draw out my savings and buy a few shares. Does Vandering Enterprises sell stock?"

"Not all of the Vandering companies. But on my advice Howard went public with some of them."

"What's going public?"

"Listen," he said severely, "if you don't know even that, stay out of the market. Come to think of it, stay out of it anyway. It's not for people. It's for bulls and bears. And sharks."

"Like you?"

"Like me." The waiter had reappeared. Dan took the menu card handed to him and then looked across at Ellen. "What would you like for dessert?"

"Thank you, but I don't care for dessert."

"Then I don't either." Handing the menu back to the waiter, he said, "Two coffees."

A few minutes later, out on the sidewalk, Dan Reardon hailed a cab. As it angled toward the curb, he said, "I have to fly down to Florida tomorrow. Trouble in a pre-fab company there. But may I call you when I get back?"

"You may. I'm in the book under E. B. Stacey. B for Beatrice."

He opened the cab door for her. When she was seated, he closed the door and asked, "What's your address?"

She gave it to him. Walking to the front of the cab, he repeated the address, handed the driver a bill, and said, "Give the young lady a nice safe ride."

"Yes, *sir!*"

From the driver's enthusiasm, she knew Dan must have given him a five-dollar bill for a four-block ride. For a moment she thought of protesting. Then she leaned back and, as the cab pulled away, smiled her thanks at the man standing on the curb. Perhaps when he was a little boy growing up in that Brooklyn slum, he had dreamed of having a cab driver say, "Yes, *sir!*" in just that tone.

As she looked at the Madison Avenue sidewalk crowd moving along through the unseasonably hot sunlight, she realized that she was still smiling. She had enjoyed that lunch. The last of her muscular stiffness seemed gone. And she had lost, for some reason she couldn't define, not only all doubt that the accident hadn't been just that, but even the faint uneasiness she had felt at intervals ever since she had found the drug-dazed child on the terrace.

nine

Len Vandering had meant to have his air conditioner repaired before warm weather began. But the sudden onslaught of heat had caught him by surprise. Stripped to the waist, he stood in the gray light pouring down through the skylight, frowned at the easel-propped canvas before him, and then made a quick brush stroke.

In the living room behind him, the phone shrilled. Damn! Usually he muffled the phone before starting work, but this time he had forgotten. He tried to ignore the phone for several rings. Then, laying the brush in its slot at the base of the easel, he went in to answer.

"Leonard? Dan Reardon here. Am I interrupting something?"

"That's all right," Len said, in a tone which conveyed that it wasn't.

"I just phoned Howard in Toledo. He had a message for you. It's about that painting of yours which was in *Life* three weeks ago. If it isn't sold, a friend of Howard's out in Ohio wants to buy it. He'll be in town next week."

"All right. I'll call the gallery. And thanks."

"Think nothing of it. Incidentally, I just had lunch with

80

a friend of yours."

God, Leonard thought. Big business types were always moaning about the pressure of their lives. And yet they would call up someone who really did work hard and waste his time with chit-chat.

"What friend?"

"Ellen Stacey."

Len's grip on the phone tightened. He said coolly, "Oh?"

"She's great, isn't she? Not just her looks, although she's okay in that department, too. But she's so sort of gentle and—well, damned nice."

"I agree. But I wouldn't have thought she was your type." He had tried to speak casually, but his words held an edge.

Dan reacted to it. "What the hell do you know about my type? Just because you see me around with call girls sometimes doesn't mean I can't appreciate someone like Ellen."

"My mistake." Then, forcing himself to sound pleasant, "How's Vandering Enterprises doing?"

"Oh, managing to stay afloat." Reardon too had moderated his tone. "Well, see you around, fella."

"Sure. So long."

He went into his studio, picked up the brush, and then, after a moment, threw it down. His concentration had been ruined. Damn that interfering bastard. Interfering in more ways than one.

Returning to the living room, he stood at the window and stared down at two stout women who sat on the steps of the tenement across the street, fanning themselves with what looked like folded sections of the *Daily News*.

When he'd phoned her that morning, Ellen had told him that she didn't feel up to seeing anyone. And yet an hour or so later she was sitting in some restaurant with that cheap wheeler-dealer. And to judge by what he had said on the phone, he would try to see her again.

Why had she gone to lunch with him? Some women, he knew, would feel a masochistic attraction to the street tough who lurked behind that tanned, expensively barbered and tailored exterior. Ellen hadn't appeared to be that type of woman, but perhaps she was.

Anyway, it didn't look good—not at all good.

Wearing a blue robe over her slip, Cecily also stared out a window, even though she was supposed to be lying on that narrow bed across the room. "If you take a nice nap," the nurse had said, the gray-haired one with granny glasses, "you'll feel much better."

As a matter of fact, at the moment Cecily felt neither good nor bad. This was one of those times when she thought of herself as a glass of water—tasteless, colorless, almost a nothing.

Such times were all right. The bad times were when she felt like that ugly brown puddle, all that had been left of that beautiful little pool in the woods near the house in the Hamptons.

She and her father had discovered it one springtime morning—the last springtime before the divorce. She was five then. In those days she must have been one of those crazy little kids who are always laughing, because her father had called her Gertie the Girl Gurgler. She remembered laughing at the way the faintly stirred waters of the pool—it was being fed by a spring, her father told her—had made her reflection waver. The reflected sky had wavered too, and a branch of a maple tree, strung with un-

82

opened buds like fat red beads.

The next season she and her mother had driven out to the house alone, except for the Lindquists. While the baggage was being carried indoors, Cecily had slipped away to look at the pool.

Something had happened to it. Perhaps the spring had dried up. Anyway, it had shrunk to an ugly brown puddle, no larger than ones you find on Central Park paths when the snow begins to melt. She had thought, "That's me down there." Like the pool, she had become something muddy and sad and worthless.

It was the divorce that had made her feel like the brown puddle. After her father had moved out of the apartment, her mother had tried to explain it to her. "You must never blame your father," she had said. "It was just that we couldn't get along." And her father, the first weekend she spent at his new Central Park South apartment, had told her, "None of this was your mother's fault, honey."

And so Cecily had known, even though of course neither of them would tell her so, that it was because of her they couldn't "get along." Somehow, she had become unlovable, at least to her father. Otherwise he wouldn't have left her. For a long time—oh, maybe until she was almost seven—she had tried to win him back by telling him she would bake cookies for him on her toy stove, and dumb things like that.

Standing there beside the window, she suddenly stiffened. Five stories below and across the street, a man had stopped in the dappled shadow of a tree to light a cigarette. Was he one of them? The tall, thin one? If he looked up at the window . . .

He snapped his lighter shut, dropped it into a coat pocket, and walked on. Not one of them, just a man on the street.

But she was beginning to have that brown-puddle feeling so strongly that her body felt heavy. Crossing the room, she lay down on the bed and stared at the ceiling.

For quite a while now, she had known that it wasn't just the divorce that caused the sadness. Lots of kids had divorced parents. By the time she was nine, she had realized that. No, what caused the sadness was something that rhymed with it. Badness. Perhaps her father long ago had sensed the badness in her, without realizing it. Perhaps even if he didn't know it, it was what made him feel he couldn't go on living with her and her mother. Anway, the badness was there. Those two men had seen it instantly, that first time, a year and a half ago, when they had approached her there in the aquarium. They had known she would use the stuff in those little packets.

Sometimes she wondered if they had known about those marijuana cigarettes she had found in Uncle Len's kitchen. She couldn't see how they could have known, but they might have.

Not that those had been the first cigarettes she had ever smoked. The winter she was eight, she had taken cigarettes from a crystal box in the living room a few times when no one else was in the apartment, and tried to smoke. She hadn't liked it, and so, after three or four attempts, she had stopped doing it.

But the marijuana cigarettes had been something else. She had known they were marijuana almost as soon as her hand, fishing around in that cookie jar, had closed around them and drawn them out. Their paper was brown and they had a lumpy, homemade look, like those she had seen in a magazine illustration.

84

That night in her room, with the light out and the windows wide open, she had lit one of the lumpy cigarettes. Sitting in bed with updrawn knees, flicking the ash into one of the doll plates she sometimes still played with, she waited. At last, disappointed, she carried the doll plate into the small adjoining bathroom and flushed the ashes and the short stub away. But as she rinsed the plate at the wash basin, she recalled something that a classmate, Carol Stapleton, had told her. Carol had heard her brother, the one who went to Brown, telling a friend over the phone that the first time he'd tried grass he hadn't felt a thing. But the second time . . .

It was like that for her. The next night while she sat in bed in her darkened room intermittently seeing her reflected face, lit by the cigarette's glow, in her dressing table mirror, she had felt a sense of peace stealing over her. She knew the sadness was still there, but it didn't hurt much. When there was less than half an inch of the cylinder left, she carried it into the bathroom.

Perhaps the Lindquists, whose room was across the hall from hers, had caught a whiff of the smoke. Perhaps Mrs. Lindquist, cleaning Cecily's bathroom, had found some telltale fibers. Whatever the reason, within a minute or two after Cecily had lit a cigarette the third night, the door opened and the overhead light blazed on. Her mother stood there, blue eyes stricken in her white face.

Her mother that night, and her father the next afternoon, talked to her gently, sorrowfully. Whatever anger they felt seemed to be directed toward Uncle Len. She promised both her parents that she would never touch marijuana again. Sometimes the memory of that lulling pace made her want to break her promise. Perhaps she could suggest to Carol

85

that she might sneak some of her brother's grass the next time he was home. But she hadn't suggested it. For one thing, there was her promise. For another, Carol wasn't really her friend. None of the girls seemed to want to be her friend, except for a homely, stuttering Greek girl who had attended Mainwaring for a few months. And even then Cecily had heard other girls giggling one day over a rhyme they had made up: "Christina, the stuttering Greek, and Cecily, the silent freak."

Christina had already transferred to a Connecticut school by the time, the winter before last, when Cecily had gone with her natural history class to the aquarium. Miss Beazley, as always, had tried to keep the class together—"Jennifer, Alice, don't go on ahead like that! And you girls back there, don't dawdle!"—but, as always, Miss Beazley had failed.

Cecily was far behind any of the others, exchanging stares with a black-and-white striped fish in a tank, when she became vaguely aware that two men stood beside her. One of them said, "Kid."

She looked up. He was a tall man in a gray felt hat. He smiled, revealing front teeth that overlapped slightly. The other man, short and stocky, stood with his gaze fixed on Miss Beazley and the group of girls around her, twenty yards or so away up the long aisle between the rows of tanks.

The tall man said, "I just put something in your purse, kid. Nose candy." He winked at her. "You sniff it. It's better than airplane glue, or hair spray, or anything like that."

Startled and frightened, she looked down at her red shoulder bag. Its clasp was undone.

"And, kid."

She looked up. He wasn't smiling now. "Don't tell anybody. You do, and we'll fix you. The police won't know how to find us, but we know how to find you, anytime we want. Remember that."

She stared dumbly up at him. Nose candy. She knew what that meant. Heroin. She had seen this TV show where some kids—big kids, teen-agers—had sat with their backs to the camera and talked about sniffing nose candy. She felt fear, and repulsion, and above all, a burning shame. Why had they picked her out? Because they had seen the badness. One look, and they had known.

"Cecily!" Miss Beazley had called. "What are you doing back there? Come on."

The tall man said, staring at the striped fish, "Remember, kid."

Moving numbly up the aisle, Cecily knew that she would never tell. Not because of the fear, but the shame.

She waited until she was home in her room before she looked in her handbag. She drew out a white letter-sized envelope, folded over once. Inside it were three little packets of what looked like heavy cellophane, filled with white powder. Her hands felt cold and clumsy as she restored the little packets to the envelope, opened the second drawer of her bureau, lifted a pile of folded school blouses, and slipped the envelope beneath the scented paper that lined the drawer.

For a full week she left it there. It would have been easy to get rid of it. Sometimes in class, remembering the packets and feeling her face grow hot with the shame of that moment in the aquarium, she would think, "I'll get rid of it when I go home." But once in her room, all she would do was to lift the pile of blouses and stare, transfixed, at the faintly raised place in the paper lining. It was like that bottle labeled, "Drink me," the one that fascinated Alice. . . .

Friday of that week was a very bad day. For one thing, the first Santas had appeared on the street. Each year she had seemed to get the brown-puddle feeling stronger and stronger when the Santas started ringing their bells. Since she always got lots of Christmas presents, she didn't know why the Santas made her feel sad, but they did. Then, when she got home, she found Dale Haylock about to leave. Even though he smiled at her, she could see the anger in his eyes—blue eyes of that light shade that often goes with red hair. She knew why he was angry. Mother, who had once thought of marrying Dale—she had told Cecily so at the time—had decided not to. And Dale wouldn't accept that.

But the worst thing had happened at dinner. In March, her mother had told her, she was going to Mexico for six weeks. "You'll be fine, darling. Cousin Martha will come to stay with you."

Cecily felt as if a heavy weight had pressed down on her chest. The thought of six weeks alone with Cousin Martha seemed more than she could bear. Fat Cousin Martha, with wrinkled eyelids over little gray eyes, and the black button of a hearing aid in her left ear.

Cecily's mother thought that Cousin Martha felt kindly toward her, and liked coming to this apartment, and wearing the mink coat, once Mother's, that was older than Cecily herself. But Cecily had seen Cousin Martha looking at Mother when Mother didn't know it, and so she knew that Cousin Martha didn't like Mother at all.

After dinner that night, her mother went out. Walking down the hall, Cecily heard the subdued murmur of a TV set from behind the Lindquists' door. She went into her room, undressed and put on her nightgown, and opened the bureau drawer.

Sitting on the edge of her bed, with a carefully unfolded transparent packet on her palm, she sniffed the white powder just as she sniffed a camphor stick when she had a cold, holding a finger against one nostril and then the other. About to sneeze, she turned her head in time to save the remaining powder on the outspread packet.

Seconds after she had placed the refolded packet under the drawer lining and slipped into bed, she learned that the man in the aquarium had spoken truly. Moments ago she had felt small and chilled and lonely, like someone trudging across a bleak, endless plain under a gray sky. But now it was as if clouds had opened and golden sunlight had flooded down, wrapping her in warm well-being, so that the bad things didn't matter—not that rhyme about Cecily, the silent freak, not her mother's Mexico trip next March, not even the divorce.

After a while the elation faded, leaving her with a peaceful drowsiness. She moved farther down in the bed and drew the blankets up to her chin.

And yet she didn't even touch the little packets in the drawer again for many weeks, because at lunch the next day—the last Saturday of the month, which she always spent with her father—she met her father's new friend, Amy Thornhill.

Amy wasn't pretty, at least nowhere near as pretty as Mother. But she had a throaty voice that was like music, and blue eyes that held a warm gentleness. What was more, unlike other grownups, she seemed to think of Cecily as a person in her own right, someone to talk to, not just Howard Vandering's daughter, to be asked the same old questions—Do you like school? What's your favorite subject?—and then ignored for the rest of the meal. Before the luncheon was over, she had invited Cecily to go ice skating with her the next Saturday.

After lunch their taxi dropped Amy at her hairdresser's. As Cecily and her father traveled north along Fifth Avenue, he asked, "Well, how do you like her?" He looked happier, she noticed, than she could ever remember him looking.

"I like her a lot, Daddy."

He put his arm around her shoulders and squeezed. "Enough that you wouldn't mind having her as a stepmother? If she'll marry me, that is."

She sat very still in the circle of his arm. If he married Amy, there would no longer be a chance that he would come back to the apartment to live. But then, a long time ago she had given up all but a little shred of that hope.

And on the weekends she spent at his apartment, the three of them would be like a real family. At dinner there would be her father at one end of the table, and Amy at the other, and herself in the middle. They would go lots of places together. And at Christmas, she thought—staring at the Santa outside Bergdorf's, and not minding the sight of him—they would get a very big tree, and all three trim it.

"Daddy, please ask her. She won't turn you down."

When her father left her at the Fifth Avenue apartment Sunday night, she described Amy to her mother. Even though she was aware of the hurt in her mother's lovely eyes, contradicted by her smile, she couldn't keep the enthusiasm out of her voice.

At last her mother said, still smiling, "It's good to see you so excited about someone, darling. You're usually such a little sobersides. Yes, you can go skating with her. If your father likes her, she must be all right."

It wasn't until after she had gone to bed that Cecily thought of the packets in her bureau drawer. She didn't want the white powder. She wanted to lie here and think of her father and Amy and herself having dinner together.

Flush the white powder away?

No.

Grownups were not dependable. Amy might decide that she, Cecily, was a nuisance. Or her father and Amy might quarrel. And once again, that unbearable sadness might descend.

But apparently Amy Thornhill never did find her a nuisance. They had a glorious, giggling time on the rink the next Saturday, even though Amy sat down hard three times. ("Never mind," she said. "It's good for the hips.") After that they went skating, or shopping, or to a matinee every weekend, even those weekends when Cecily didn't stay with her father.

Several times during those winter weeks, a shadow fell across her cautiously unfolding sense of happiness. On four different occasions as she stared out the apartment's front window after school, she thought she saw one of the men from the aquarium on the sidewalk across the street, moving slowly along the high stone wall that bordered Central Park. Once the man was tall and thin, like the one who had spoken to her. The other three times the pedestrian moving along through the winter dusk had resembled his stocky, silent companion. Each time, feeling her hands

91

turn cold, she had tried to reassure herself that it wasn't one of them. After all, there were thousands of tall, thin men, and short, wide-shouldered ones.

In March her mother went to Mexico, leaving Cousin Martha in charge of the apartment. With the weekend to look forward to, she found she didn't mind Cousin Martha too much, not even when she saw her sniff the bottles on Mother's dressing table, wrinkling her nose as if the bottles held something nasty instead of perfume, or staring enviously at the still life painting in the foyer which hid the safe where Mother kept her jewelry. After all, you couldn't blame Cousin Martha for feeling envious. Before her late husband had lost all his money, she, too, had owned jewelry. Now the only jewelry she had was the big diamond solitaire on her pudgy left hand. ("But it's worth thousands," she had once told Cecily with sour triumph. "It's more valuable than any single ring of your mother's.")

When Cecily came home from school the first Friday after her mother's departure, Cousin Martha said, "Miss Thornhill called."

Apprehension clutched Cecily. Maybe Amy couldn't make it tomorrow. And they had planned such a wonderful afternoon, lunch at the Central Park cafeteria, and then the zoo. "What did Amy want?"

"She wants me to have lunch with you two tomorrow. We're to meet her by the Alice in Wonderland statue at one o'clock and then walk to the cafeteria."

"Why?" Cecily asked, too dismayed to remember her manners. "Why did she ask you?"

"Because she's considerate, that's why. She can understand how I'd get lonely, sitting here in an apartment that isn't my own. She may be just a working girl, but she's a real lady, not like some I could mention."

Feeling resigned, Cecily went to her room and studied her American history text until dinnertime.

Cousin Martha was at first absent at the breakfast table the next morning, and when she finally did appear, she was red-nosed and watery-eyed. "Dambed cold," she explained.

"I'm sorry."

But Cecily's face must have betrayed her, because Cousin Martha said, with a tight little smile, "Oh, I'll be able to go. I took cold pills. I'll be all right by lunchtime."

She wasn't, though. When Cecily, dressed in a warm coat and fur hood, came into the living room a few minutes before one, she found Cousin Martha on a yellow satin love seat, her face glum as she flipped the pages of a magazine.

"I feel awful. Tell Mizz Thornhill I'd like a raincheck."

"You mean I can walk over there by myself?"

"Whad else would I mean?"

As long as Cecily could remember, the park stretching away beyond the stone wall across the avenue had been semi-forbidden territory. She had gone there with nursemaids, and with one or both of her parents, and with classmates for riding lessons along the bridle paths. But she had never gone there alone.

She hesitated only a few seconds. Amy would be waiting. " 'By," she said, and hurried out lest Cousin Martha suddenly realize that Central Park wasn't the safest place in the world for an unaccompanied ten-year-old. Walking to the corner, she crossed the avenue to the park's Seventyninth Street entrance.

Dazzling in the sunlight, snow from the last big storm blanketed the park. A hill just ahead swarmed with kids, from two-year-olds to teen-agers, who hurtled down the slope on sleds and flying saucers. With an exhilarated sense of freedom, Cecily turned left onto a broad path, and then left again onto a narrower one that led down to the Alice in Wonderland statue.

"Hello, kid."

Her heart gave a painful thud. Stopping short, she looked up into the face of the tall man, and then darted a glance at the other one. He stood a few feet away, hands thrust in the slanted pockets of his duffle coat, his watchful gaze directed up the path.

She was aware that the tall man's hand had made a slight movement. "We figured you must be out of nose candy about now. Look in your pocket when you get home. We gave you more this time." He paused, and then added, "Go on being a good kid. Keep your mouth shut, and you'll never run short."

"Cecily!"

Her hand snapped around. Amy stood at the foot of the path leading up from the Alice statue.

"Kid," the man muttered. That was all. But the look he gave her, before he turned away and joined his companion striding briskly up the path, held such threat that her whole body turned cold.

Looking back to Amy, she saw that the woman moved toward her now, an anxious smile on her lips. Cecily's hand darted into her pocket, closed around crackling paper. Get rid of it, get rid of it! She took a step forward, pretending to stumble, and fell sidewise, plunging her left arm deep into a snow-laden rhododendron bush. When she scrambled to her feet, her left hand was empty.

Amy crouched beside her, brushing snow from Cecily's

coat with a mittened hand. "Did you hurt yourself?"

"No, I'm fine."

"Look, you scratched your wrist!"

"It's all right. It isn't even bleeding." Get Amy away from that bush. "I'll wash it when we get to the cafeteria."

Amy got to her feet. "Where's Mrs. Barlow?"

"She has a cold," Cecily said, starting down the path.

Amy fell into step beside her. "That's too bad." Then, in a casual tone: "What was that man saying to you."

After a moment Cecily answered, "He's lost his dog."

"Oh? Why did he tell you about it?"

"He wondered if I'd seen it."

"What kind of a dog was it?"

"German shepherd. His name is Leo."

"Why, isn't that a coincidence! Your father mentioned that he once had a German shepherd who was still alive when you were a little girl. Wasn't his name Leo?"

"Yes," she answered miserably.

Amy dropped the subject then. But when they had almost finished their veal cutlet and salad in the crowded, noisy cafeteria, she said, "Dear, didn't I see that man put something in your pocket?"

Cecily's fingers tightened around her glass of milk. "No."

"But, Cecily! I'm sure I did."

"Oh, yes. I forgot. He gave me his telephone number, in case I saw his dog."

"Would you mind showing me the number?"

Getting up, Cecily lifted her coat from the chairback and plunged her hand into the left-hand pocket and then the right. "It isn't here. It must have fallen out, somehow."

She handed the coat to Amy. After dipping her hand into the pockets, Amy gave the coat back to her and said,

95

"Yes, it must have fallen out. Sit down, dear, and finish your lunch."

For the first time since she had known her, Cecily wanted to get away from Amy. Even as they looked at her favorite zoo animal, the huge buffalo who had always seemed to her noble and lonely and sad, like some imprisoned black king, she was thinking of those packets of white powder in her bureau drawer. How could she have been silly enough to keep them all this time? She had to get rid of them. If anyone ever found them, Amy might hear of it, and that would be more than Cecily could bear.

Shortly after three o'clock, Amy walked with her to the Fifth Avenue apartment house and said good-by. Upstairs, Cecily found Cousin Martha, Kleenex in hand, watching a game show on the portable TV set she had placed atop one of the exquisitely inlaid French tables. "Yes, we had a good time," she said, in answer to Cousin Martha's question. Walking back to her room, she took the packets from the bureau drawer, carried them into the bathroom, and flushed their contents away. The plastic containers, she thought, as she watched the water swirl into the bowl, could be dropped into a litter basket on her way to school Monday.

The next afternoon, Sunday, as she sat studying French verbs in her room, the door opened and Cousin Martha said, her face strangely expressionless, "Your father's here."

Closing her French text, Cecily walked out into the hall in time to see Cousin Martha disappear inside the bedroom that was temporarily hers. Feeling a strange dread, Cecily moved on to the living room.

Her father looked old—terribly old. Pulling her down beside him on a sofa, he put his arms around her and said, "Darling, something has happened to Amy."

Cold and dumb with shock, she listened. Amy was dead. Since the news would be in the papers and on TV, it was better that she know about it right now. Thieves had broken in and killed her as she lay asleep. "She didn't suffer. That's the one thing we can comfort ourselves with. I'm sorry I can't stay now, honey. The police want to talk to me again. But Cousin Martha is waiting for you in her room. She knows about it."

He kissed her cheek, which was so numb it scarcely felt his lips, and moved toward the foyer. Halfway there, he stopped and turned around. "What with this terrible thing, I'd almost forgotten. But Amy phoned me late yesterday afternoon. She sounded worried, and I caught the impression it had something to do with you."

With her. The two men on the path. Amy had wanted to tell Cecily's father about them. They had been afraid she might do that, and so they had killed her. It wasn't thieves who had done it. It was those two men. So it was almost as if she herself had killed Amy.

"Do you have any idea what she could have wanted to tell me?"

Cecily shook her head. That day at the aquarium, the tall man had said, "We'll know how to find you, anytime." And they had known, and they'd known how to find Amy, and they would know how to find her mother or her father.

He said heavily, "Well, I guess I'll never know what it was. I'll phone you tomorrow, honey."

She waited until she heard the click of the closing front door. Then she went down the hall. But she didn't stop at Cousin Martha's room. Instead she put on her coat and hood, slipped out of the apartment, and crossed to the park.

For a Sunday afternoon, the park was quite empty. Already light was dying out of the gray sky, the bare trees writhed in a cold northwest wind, and melted snow on the path was turning to ice. She hurried past the hill, where only one small boy toiled up the slope beside his sled-pulling father, took the path that led to the Alice statue, and stopped beside the rhododendron bush.

After looking up and down the empty path, she crouched, and then thrust her hand deep among the stiff branches and shiny leaves. Her fingers closed around the paper envelope. As she got to her feet and shoved the envelope deep in her pocket, she saw that it was soggy and mud-streaked. But surely the powder in those tightly sealed plastic packets would be all right.

No need to wait until she got home before escaping from this pain, this unbearable knowledge that it was because of her that her friend had been killed. She walked on down the path, entered a restroom, and, behind the latched door of a booth, opened one of the five packets inside the envelope.

ten

Several mornings during the weeks that followed, Cecily awoke feeling so heavy of limb and so low in spirit that she asked Cousin Martha to phone the school that she was sick. And even when she did go to school, she found it hard to take an interest in the War of 1812, or color slides of French Impressionist pictures.

One afternoon her English teacher asked her to stay after class. "Cecily, do you realize that I'm going to have to give you a D at midterm?"

"I'm sorry, Miss Haynes."

"Don't you feel well? You've been looking awfully thin and pale these past few weeks. Have you seen a doctor?"

"Oh, yes," she lied. "Dr. Carson says I'm rundown. He's giving me a tonic."

Less than a week later, she actually did see him. Her mother, lovely and delicately tanned, walked into the apartment late one afternoon, looked at Cecily, and gathered her anxiously close. Half an hour later, Cecily heard her phoning Dr. Carson.

The next morning, an April day a little more than a year ago, he had examined her in his office here at the clinic.

After a while, he and her mother had gone into another room. When he returned, smiling, he told Cecily that she was to spend a few days at the clinic so he could "run some tests."

They had put her in a different room, that first time—one overlooking the courtyard. The next morning, as she stood at the window staring down at gravel walks bordered with butter-yellow forsythia, there had been a knock at the door. A second later her mother and Dr. Carson came in. One look at their faces told her that they had found what little was left of the powder, there in the last of the five packets in her bureau drawer. Seeing the pain and terror in her mother's face, and, a few hours later, in her father's, she had vowed that she would never touch any of that white powder again.

The next two days were bad—very bad. Dr. Carson questioned her, and her mother and father. Even Mrs. Baron, headmistress of the Mainwaring School and, so the girls said, niece of its founder, came to the clinic, her face holding a fear which Cecily knew was far more for the school than for Cecily herself. Sitting on a straight chair in her room, she stuck to her story with quiet, desperate stubbornness: she had found the heroin in a bush in Central Park.

On the third day her mother had come into the room wearing a too-bright smile. Everything had been arranged. She and Cecily would go to Europe right away, and spend four months there.

Europe had been all right—sometimes better than all right. Sometimes, standing in a flower-strewn Swiss meadow, or jolting along an Irish road in a charabanc, she almost forgot about Amy's death, and the two men, and the indefinable badness in herself that had drawn them to her.

After she and her mother returned to New York, she had worked hard with a tutor to make up for lost class time. When she had passed the examination which would enable her to return to the Mainwaring School in the fall, her mother told her that from now on there would be a new arrangement. Either her mother or Lindquist would drive her to school in the morning and pick her up in the afternoon. Cecily didn't ask why. She knew why. And she was grateful. She had dreaded the thought of walking the few blocks between the apartment and the school, when at any moment those two might appear beside her.

She hadn't seen them again, not for sure, all through the fall and winter, even though, with a frightened fascination, she kept looking for them, drifting to the apartment windows to stare down at the opposite side of the street, scanning the sidewalk crowd as she and her mother rode downtown in a taxi, and the faces of other patrons in the restaurants where she and her father lunched or dined on her weekends with him. Gradually she stopped looking. Sometimes days would pass without her even thinking of them. And when she did think of them, it was with a growing hope that the badness in her, which had attracted them, somehow had disappeared.

At noon last Monday, she had walked back along the school's downstairs corridor to a row of lockers. As she inserted her key and swung the steel door back, she was vaguely aware that a stocky man, carrying the sort of tool kit telephone repairmen use, moved toward her from the shadowy area beyond the row of lockers. Pausing beside

101

her for an instant, he dropped a white envelope at her feet, and then moved rapidly toward the building's front door.

Helplessly, like one caught in a bad dream, she bent and picked up the envelope, and then turned to look along the corridor. Except for two older girls, chattering about the last Junior Assembly as they opened their own lockers, the hall was now empty. She reached into the locker for her shoulder bag of fringed suede, put the envelope into it, and slipped the strap over her shoulder. After relocking the steel cabinet, she walked past the two girls and out into the cold sunlight.

Just as she reached the corner of Madison Avenue, a bus pulled up at the curb. She boarded it, neither knowing nor caring where it went. For a long time she rode, empty of thought, only dimly conscious of the traffic and sidewalk crowds and store fronts outside the window, and of the elderly woman, shabbily dressed in an old coat and with a man's muffler knotted beneath her chin, who sat beside her. The bus's tires crunched over gravel. "Fort Tyron Park," the driver said. "Cloisters Museum. This is the end of the line, folks."

She left the bus and stood there on the gravel, while other passengers streamed past her toward a stone building, dark against the cold blue sky. The Cloisters. Why, she had been here years and years ago, when she was six. No, younger, because both Mother and Daddy had been with her that day.

The protective numbness dissolved. Pain battered her. The divorce. Amy. The badness inside herself that hadn't gone away, after all.

Going into the building, she locked herself in a restroom cubicle. A few minutes later she walked along a flagstoned corridor. The wooden statues of saints she passed were not real. Neither was the splash of fountains. The only reality was the glow spreading through her. She walked out onto a deserted terrace and, squinting against painfully bright sunlight, stared at the New Jersey shore. Then, suddenly drowsy, she moved over to one corner of the terrace, curled up on the flagstones, and leaned her cheek against the museum wall.

Sometime later she had awakened in a taxi. Amy seemed to be riding beside her, face turned toward the window. She had said, with fearful joy, "Amy?" and the lady had turned around.

She was not Amy. She was younger and prettier, and her hair was lighter. But something warm and soft and concerned in the lady's eyes reminded her so strongly of Amy that she felt a rush of fear for her. What had she said to the lady? Stay away from me? Something like that.

And then she was in the apartment along with the lady, and Dr. Carson, and Mother, who had put her arms around her. . . .

The door opened. The plump nurse thrust her white-capped head around the door's edge and then, smiling, came into the room.

"So we're awake, are we?"

"Yes."

"Did you have a nice nap?"

"Yes," Cecily said.

eleven

As it turned out, Ellen's excuse to Len Vandering that she would be busy over the next few days became a valid one. To her surprised pleasure, the sponsor had liked the coffee commercial "demo," or demonstration film, which she had considered a failure. She spent all day Friday and Saturday on the set.

After her hard work, Sunday morning's leisure seemed especially blissful. As she sat beside the window, a second cup of coffee on the little folding table beside her, she wondered what gave Sundays in New York their special quality. Part of it, surely, was that on Sundays the roar of traffic above and below ground sank to a subdued hum. Part of it, too, was the awesome amount of reading matter supplied by the Sunday *Times,* various sections of which were strewn in cheerful disorder around her feet. But there was some other quality not shared by any other city she had ever been in—something indefinable and yet so recognizable that she felt sure that if she awoke from a long coma on Sunday, she would know instantly that she was in New York, and that it was the seventh day of the week.

The phone rang. Crossing the room, she lifted it from

its cradle.

"Miss Stacey? This is Howard Vandering. I'm not calling too early, am I?"

"Not at all." She glanced at the clock. Eleven-thirty. Perhaps he thought she had danced until all hours at someplace like the Rainbow Grill the night before, whereas the unglamorous truth was that she had fallen into bed, exhausted, at nine o'clock.

"Dan Reardon tells me you had what might have been a very serious accident last Wednesday night."

Hard work these past two days had almost banished the incident from her mind. "The fall wouldn't have been serious," she said lightly, "just fatal. But I didn't fall, and I feel fine now."

"That's good to hear. Miss Stacey, would you do me a great favor? I'm taking Cecily to the Plaza at two this afternoon. Would you meet us in the Palm Court?"

She hesitated, feeling the ambivalence the child had aroused in her almost from the first. On the one hand, she felt compassion, even tenderness. On the other, there was this reluctance to complicate her sometimes hard-working and always economically precarious life with someone else's child, and an emotionally disturbed child at that.

"I don't know, Mr. Vandering. For one thing, I don't think Mrs. Vandering wants me to see Cecily again. In fact, she made that quite clear last Monday."

"She feels differently now. When I talked to her on the phone this morning, she said that since Cecily seems to remember you favorably, you might be able to help her. As for her attitude when you brought Cecily home last Monday —well, of course she's afraid of publicity."

But since I haven't yet called the *Daily News,* Ellen

105

thought, she's willing to take a chance. Aloud she said, "Just why do you want me to join you and Cecily, Mr. Vandering?"

"I hope she'll come to think of you as a friend—someone she'll want to confide in."

"She already has," Ellen reminded him dryly. "She told me of a mysteriously generous 'they' who gave away heroin."

"I know, I know. And the story she tells us is equally nonsensical. Just as she did the first time this happened, she insists that she found the packets under a bush."

It was almost certain, Ellen reflected, that Cecily realized no one could believe that. Pity stabbed her as she thought of the child, desperately repeating that absurd explanation. Why had she? Out of misguided loyalty to some classmate? Or, sickening thought, out of terror that her supplies might be cut off?

Suddenly Ellen's resistance collapsed. Someone, somehow, had to try to get the truth out of Cecily, or that child, with her curly dark hair and her gray, lost-looking eyes, would never reach normal adulthood. "All right, I'll meet you. Has anyone told her that I am an actress?"

"I don't think so. I know I haven't."

"Well, please don't. I have an idea about it."

When she walked into the old-world elegance of Palm Court—gilded pillars, potted palms, and a string ensemble playing *Artist's Life*—Howard and Cecily Vandering were waiting. He got to his feet as she threaded her way through the sedate Sunday crowd of cocktail drinkers (adults of all ages), Shirley Temple drinkers (children), and a few tea drinkers (mostly white-haired dowagers). When she was close to the table, she saw that Cecily's glass contained a rosy Shirley Temple, and her father's what looked like Scotch and soda.

She greeted Howard Vandering, shook hands with him, and sat down in the chair a waiter had pulled out for her. Only then did she smile at Cecily. The small face was no longer dazed, but white and set and guarded. "Hello, Cecily. How are you?"

The young voice sounded infinitely remote. "I'm fine, thank you."

Her father asked, "What will you have to drink, Miss Stacey?"

"Tea, if you don't mind."

Howard Vandering gave the order. When the waiter had gone, Ellen said, "You see, I want to keep my mind clear. I intend to study some lines tonight." That wasn't entirely untrue. She might glance over *Barefoot,* just in case she was again asked to play the lead on the summer circuit.

Howard Vandering picked up his cue. "That's right, you're an actress, aren't you? TV commercials, isn't it?"

"I do quite a few."

"And didn't you mention movies?"

"Yes, I sometimes work in movies."

The silence lengthened. The waiter placed a cup and saucer and a small white china teapot before Ellen and then withdrew. At last Cecily asked, "Do you know Barbra Streisand?"

Ellen felt triumph. It had worked. No matter how withdrawn and frightened, Cecily had at least some of a normal youngster's interest in movie stars. "As a matter of fact, I do. I worked in two of her pictures."

Cecily was silent for a few moments. Then she asked, almost as if against her will, "Which ones?"

107

"Hello, Dolly and *On a Clear Day."*

Again a pause. "Do you know Robert Redford?"

"Oh, do you like him, too? I've met him at a couple of parties."

Howard Vandering looked at his watch. "Good Lord, I didn't know it was so late. You two young ladies will excuse me, won't you?" He rose. "I have an appointment."

His daughter said swiftly, "I'll go with you, Daddy."

"No, darling." He took out his wallet. "Miss Stacey will see you to my place. But you're the hostess." He tucked a bill under her soda glass. "That's for the check."

"Please, Daddy." Her face was frightened and accusatory. She recognized a put-up job when she saw one.

"Good-by, sweetie." He bent and kissed his daughter's cheek. Straightening, he looked with haggard eyes at Ellen for a moment. "Good-by, Miss Stacey," he said, and walked away.

His daughter gazed after him until he disappeared in the lobby crowd beyond the archway. Then she looked down. With dismay, Ellen saw that her expression was more remote than ever.

"Are you going to have another soda?"

A negative shake of the curly dark head.

"Well, I think I'll finish my tea." She refilled her cup from the china pot. "You were asking about Barbra Streisand. One day when there were three little dogs on the set—"

Cecily turned her face away and stared fixedly, lips compressed, at the stringed orchestra.

So Ellen could no longer hope to slip behind the barrier. She would have to try to break through, praying that the hurt to both of them would be minimal.

108

"Cecily, it's rude to turn away when someone is talking to you, and I don't think you're a rude girl. Now look at me." Then, as the child's head reluctantly turned: "You're quite right. Your father did leave us alone in the hope you would talk to me. After all, you talked to me last Monday."

No answer but a further tightening of the lips.

"When we were coming home in the cab, you thought for a moment that I was Amy. Do you remember that?"

Still no answer.

"Amy was a good friend of yours, wasn't she?"

Cecily burst out, "Why do you want to talk about Amy? My father won't ask *you* to marry him. He's away too old for you."

Ellen felt startled. Could it be that the child thought . . . ? Her gaze searched the small, tense face. No, it had been a smoke screen. The fear in Cecily's eyes didn't arise from jealousy.

"Of course your father won't want to marry me. We're not talking about your father. We're talking about you and Amy, and about me. Since Amy was your friend, why can't I be?"

No answer.

"Don't you want to have any friends, Cecily?"

The small face twisted with a pain so unchildlike, so lonely, that Ellen thought, "Oh, God! What am I doing to her?" But she mustn't stop now. She had to break through to where the child huddled, alone and stubborn and helpless.

"Is it because Amy was killed? Is that why you don't want any more friends?"

Cecily began to sob, thin shoulders hunched, head bent over her empty soda glass. Ellen said, past the hard ache in

109

her throat, "We'll go to the ladies' room. No, leave your coat there, so the waiter will know we're coming back."

As Ellen, with the weeping child walking ahead of her, moved through the maze of tables, most of the patrons looked tactfully away. In the ladies' room, a brunette woman and a teen-age girl who was probably her daughter stood in front of the long mirror. Ellen sent the woman a pleading look. The woman nodded and then said to the girl, "Come on, Pat. We're beautiful enough."

When the door had closed behind them, Ellen crouched and put her hands on the fragile, heaving shoulders. Cecily didn't move closer, but neither did she draw away. "Darling, I know you think Amy died because she was your friend. You told me that in the taxi."

The thin body stiffened.

"You don't remember telling me that, do you? But you did. And I can understand your getting such an idea. When I was about your age—no, a year older—I thought for several weeks that I'd caused the death of an aunt of mine."

A sob broke off in the middle. Ellen went on swiftly, knowing she had caught the child's attention. "My aunt had come to see us, and she made some remark about my room being a mess. I was so rude to her that when she left the house, she was still hurt and angry. On her way home, she was in a bad traffic accident. I'd heard that angry people are more apt to have car accidents, and so I thought it was my fault."

Head still bent, the child asked thickly, "Did she die?"

"No, but for a while everyone thought she was going to. She was in the hospital three weeks. Just before she was discharged, someone got around to telling me the details of the accident. A car going the other way on a divided highway had leaped the barrier and struck my aunt's car. Any car in that particular spot at that particular moment would have been struck. It was only coincidence that it happened an hour after I had been so snippy to her.

"Now I don't know what makes you think that what happened to Amy had anything to do with you," she went on. "Maybe you'll tell me someday. But the police say that robbers killed her. And the police know about these things. They're trained to know."

She read a stir of hope in the drowned-looking eyes Cecily raised to her. "And so it's silly of you to be afraid to have friends. Now let's get the face washed."

A few minutes later, as they both sat before the long mirror, Cecily asked, "Do you really want to be my friend?"

Ellen recapped her lipstick. Well, she was in for it. "Of course I do."

"Why?"

"Because I like you. And because you remind me of someone." She kept her smile steady. "Maybe I'll tell you about her someday."

Cecily drew a comb through her hair, and then laid it down on the glass-topped counter. "It isn't just because you want to ask questions?"

"There'll be no more questions," Ellen said, and meant it. In time, perhaps Cecily would volunteer the facts that the adults around her so desperately sought.

"You mean, we'll go to lunch, and things like that?"

"Yes. Of course, I've got a living to earn."

"Do people ever go on movie sets? People who aren't in the movie, I mean?"

With an inward shudder, Ellen thought of what some directors would say if she brought an eleven-year-old onto

111

a set. Still, not all of them were like that. "I think something might be arranged. Finished? All right, let's go."

They were halfway down the Plaza's broad front steps when a man climbing toward them stopped and said, "Hello! I was coming to join you."

Surprised, Ellen looked into Len's smiling face. "How did you know we were here?"

"I called my brother, and he mentioned it." He looked down at Cecily. "Hi, punkin. You're getting so pretty that for a moment I didn't know you. I thought, 'That must be some movie starlet friend of Ellen's.' "

His niece smiled faintly. "Oh, Uncle Len."

"No kidding. I was about to ask for your autograph."

"Uncle Len, that's silly." But Ellen could tell she was pleased.

He asked, "Where are you two bound for?"

Ellen said, "I'm taking Cecily to her father."

"Good. I'll walk over there with you."

They turned onto Central Park South. Along the sidewalk couples and family groups moved at a leisurely Sunday pace. At the curb, men in high silk hats sat in the driver's seat of carriages, holding the reins of sad-looking horses, and waiting for customers willing to pay six dollars for a turn through the park. A block and a half west of Fifth Avenue, Ellen and Cecily and her uncle entered an impressive apartment house lobby. At the reception desk Len phoned his brother's apartment to make sure he was there, and then turned Cecily over to the elevator man.

Returning to Ellen, he asked, "What's next on your program?"

"Home. I have weekend laundry waiting."

"Why not let it wait? The Whitney has a show of

nineteenth-century American landscapes. Later we could have dinner."

Somehow, during that affectionately teasing exchange between Len and his niece, most of Ellen's reservations about him had vanished. "All right. The laundry can wait."

Around midnight she entered her apartment, feeling the pleasant afterglow of several hours well spent. As they left the Whitney she had been aware that, thanks to Len, she knew considerably more about painting than she had when they came in. They'd had dinner at a midtown steak house, and then gone to a Village night club where the six entertainers, who improvised skits on themes suggested by the audience, were young, talented, and hilarious. By the time Ellen said good night, she'd had an uneasy sense of liking him a little more than was prudent, considering that it was only the second time she had gone out with him.

She had started to undress, when the phone rang. Dan Reardon said, "Hey, I've been calling you all afternoon and evening."

"I'm sorry. I just got in. How are you?"

"Okay. If I may be so crude, where were you?"

"The Whitney Museum. Then Danny's Hideaway, and then the Upstairs."

"Aw, come on, Ellen."

"If you wanted to know who I was with, why didn't you ask? I was with Leonard Vandering."

"I figured you might be," he said, not sounding pleased. "How do you like him by this time?"

"I like him."

"He's thirty-three. Never trust an overage bachelor, Ellen."

113

"Aren't you one?"

"Sure. That's why I tell you not to trust them."

Ellen laughed.

"What burns me," he went on, "is that I'm in town for this one evening, and I find you out with Vandering."

Ellen felt disappointment. She had found Dan stimulating company. "You're going away again?"

"Yes, I'm taking the early Metroliner to Washington tomorrow. That self-appointed consumers' champion who's gone after the automobile and breakfast food companies is now after us. He's going to tell a Congressional committee that our pre-fab houses will fall to pieces in a dozen years."

"Will they?"

"No. Fifteen years, maybe, but not a dozen."

"It's too bad you have to travel so much."

He said, after a moment, "Well, since Howard is the senior partner, he can't be away often. He has to mind the store."

Not answering, Ellen smiled. She was sure that it wasn't his more important duties that would keep the senior partner away from Washington. To judge from what she had seen of him, Howard Vandering didn't have the toughness required to defend himself before a headline-hunting Congressional committee.

"Speaking of Howard," Dan went on, "he says that you and his little girl really hit it off today."

"I think she responded somewhat."

"You're going to go on seeing her?"

"Whenever I have the time to see her."

"You've stopped worrying about that near-brodie off the balcony?"

"Yes. Nobody's tried to run me down in the street since then, or break into my apartment. I haven't even had a kooky phone call. So I've decided the trouble was that my Sign was in the wrong House the first part of this week."

"I'll go along with that. But just the same, I'd stay away from Cecily Vandering. If you get fond of her, that kid will break your heart. She won't make it. She might have, if her parents had stayed together, but they didn't. I think she must have been a doomed kid ever since the divorce."

Ellen said, not liking him as much as she had a few moments before, "I refuse to think that any eleven-year-old is doomed."

"Have it your way. Besides, the main thing bugging me isn't Cecily. It's her Uncle Len."

"What about him? If you have anything specific against him, why not say so?"

"Oh, I guess it's just that he was born with everything I've had to fight for, and he's done nothing but show his contempt for it. He even threw away his chances of inheriting his share of the Vandering money."

"What do you care? It's not as if you were paying taxes to keep him on welfare. He supports himself."

"Painting pictures. Somehow that seems a funny way for a grown man to make a living."

"Do you know what? I'll bet that someday you'll be collecting pictures, perhaps even Leonard Vandering's."

He chuckled. "You mean I'll start getting culture? Maybe so. Up until now I've been concentrating on the other fine things of life."

"Like Delphine?"

"Who? Oh, that's right. She stopped at our table in the restaurant. I told you, girls like that don't mean a thing

115

to me." He paused. "Mind if I call you up while I'm in Washington?"

"Of course not."

"Think over what I said about the Vandering kid, will you?"

"All right. I don't think I'll change my mind, though."

"No, I suppose not. I'll call you from Washington. And maybe when I get back, you'll have dinner with me."

"I'd like to very much."

twelve

During the next two weeks, Ellen took Cecily on a Saturday afternoon shopping trip, to a Sunday matinee of a Walt Disney movie, and, by special dispensation of the director, to a Brooklyn roller skating rink one night where another scene of *Farewell, Sweet Pistachio* was being shot. Cecily volunteered no information, and Ellen, true to her promise, asked no questions. What was more, the child remained quiet and withdrawn. Even on the movie set when, at Ellen's request, a well-known character actor gave Cecily his autograph, the smile with which she thanked him held only faint animation. On the other hand, she accepted each invitation with a readiness which suggested that she enjoyed Ellen's company. And Cecily's mother, obviously trying to make up for her former aloofness, thanked Ellen warmly each time she picked up Cecily at the Fifth Avenue apartment and again when she brought her home.

Also during those two weeks Ellen had dinner with Len Vandering three times, the last time at his apartment, where in the tiny but well-equipped kitchen he prepared a very creditable meal of veal paprika, glazed carrots, and green salad. Later, as they sat side by side on one of the low sofas, with Viennese schrammel music on the hi-fi, and Benedictine glasses in their hands, he said, "I had lunch with Howard today. He's damned grateful to you for taking Cecily in hand."

"All I've done is spend a little time with her."

"That's a lot. After all, you have your work."

Ellen said dryly, "What work?"

"Things are slow?"

"Very."

She'd had a total of three days' work on the skating rink set, but since then she'd received no calls. Too, the straw-hat producer who had employed her for the last three summers had decided to present a small revue the coming season. Since Ellen was neither a singer, dancer, nor comedienne, there would be no place for her in the company.

But it didn't matter too much. Residuals from that coffee commercial would bring her an adequate income for the next few months. And in the fall, work was always more plentiful.

"Just the same," he went on, "I think it damned generous of you. I like Cecily because she's my niece, but I realize she'd never win a charming child contest, not with that sad little phiz."

"I find her appealing."

He smiled. "Frustrated maternal instinct? You know, I've wondered about that. You impress me as the sort of girl who marries at twenty and has three children before she's twenty-five."

"I married at eighteen."

"Hey! You never told me you'd been married."

"You never asked."

"What became of the guy?"

She waited until she was sure her voice would remain even. "He was killed in an airplane accident. So was our little girl. She was two."

After several moments he said, "Forgive me. If I'd had the slightest idea—"

"How could you have known? Anyway, Cecily looks like Beth, or the way Beth would have by now."

"That explains a lot."

The hi-fi had shut itself off. He crossed the room, threaded several more records onto the spindle, and turned the switch. The sound of a zither, playing the *Dr. Zhivago Theme,* filled the room. Len sat down beside her, took the liqueur glass from her hand, and kissed her thoroughly. As always, she enjoyed his kiss, but now it held a new and disturbing tenderness.

Although she smiled at him when he had released her, that sense of disturbance remained. He was attractive, successful not only artistically but to at least some degree financially, and a Vandering. When and if he decided to marry, he would have an almost unlimited choice of girls. It wouldn't do for a twenty-eight-year-old actress of no particular distinction and of modest background to fall in love with him. It wouldn't do at all.

She said, still smiling, "How is your work coming?"

His own smile, quizzical but unprotesting, acknowledged the distance she had put between them. "It's going well, off and on. Today was off."

"I noticed as soon as I walked in tonight that the door to your studio was closed. It was open the first time I came here."

"I had the distinct impression that you didn't like my

119

'Family Group.' So I decided to shield you from the sight of them."

She thought of the white plaster figures standing there in the darkened studio. Were the masks in place? Or did the little boy stare up with brooding pain and envy at the beloved older brother? He had gotten it all out of his system, Len had said. But did the unfavored sibling ever really forgive the favored one?

No, better not to fall in love with Len. Like a ship venturing close to a harmless-looking iceberg, she might find herself smashed against knifelike ridges hidden beneath the water.

Two afternoons later, only a few minutes after she returned to her apartment from an Actors Equity meeting, someone pushed the downstairs button on the intercom. Unhooking the earpiece, Ellen said, "Hello."

"This is Janet Vandering, Miss Stacey. I know my dropping by is an imposition, and if you're busy, please just say so."

"I'm not."

"Then may I come up?"

"Please do." Wondering, Ellen pressed the button that released the latch on the front door.

Mrs. Vandering came in, elegant in a linen dress of that shade of beige so becoming to fragile blondes. Despite artful makeup, her face looked tired, almost haggard.

She said, glancing around, "What a pleasant room."

"Thank you," Ellen said, knowing exactly how her flowered cretonne slip covers must appear to a woman who owned eighteenth-century French furniture. "Please sit down. What can I offer you? I have some sherry."

"Oh, please! Nothing at all, thank you." She leaned forward in her chair. "I've come here about Cecily, of course."

"Is she all right?" Feeling a leap of alarm, Ellen realized, not too happily, how fond she had become of that strange child.

"Oh, yes. Or at least she's much the same as usual. She received her grades for her final examinations today. She did quite well, in spite of that week she was out of school. There will be no trouble getting her into another school in the fall, at least not from the academic standpoint."

"She isn't going back to Mainwaring?"

"No." Painful color showed in her face. "The school asked me not to enroll her."

So, Ellen thought, the school felt it couldn't overlook a second episode so potentially dangerous to its reputation, even though the child involved was a Vandering.

"But what I came to see you about," Janet Vandering hurried on, "is the coming summer. I took her to Europe last summer. For a while the results seemed to be good, but then—well, you know what happened a few weeks ago." She made a despairing gesture. "The truth is, I've lost faith in my ability to help my daughter. Besides, I'm tired, Miss Stacey. I just don't feel capable of coping with an emotionally disturbed child for the next three months."

Certainly she didn't look capable. Whether because of worry over her daughter or something else—memory of an angrily importunate Dale Haylock crossed Ellen's mind—Mrs. Vandering looked to be on the thin edge.

"And so I have this tremendous favor to ask of you. Now I know how much your career must mean to you—"

"It's been years since I thought of it as a career, Mrs. Vandering. Now it's a way of making a living."

"Your work, then. But anyway, could you possibly spend the summer with Cecily at my house on eastern Long Island? You can name your own salary. And it wouldn't be just the two of you. My cousin Martha Barlow has consented to spend the summer out there. And since I'll be closing the apartment—some friends of mine have invited me to Cape Cod—this couple I employ, the Lindquists, would look after you."

Ellen said slowly, "Why, it sounds wonderful." She thought of New York City in the summertime. The unlovely, sweating crowds in subways and buses. The heat-softened asphalt into which your heel sometimes sank, so that you literally walked out of your shoe. The icy air conditioning in restaurants and producers' offices which only made the temperature seem more torrid when you emerged into the street.

"My house is set in woodland, with a path leading down to the bay. You'd have the station wagon, of course, and so you'd be able to reach East Hampton and the other villages within a few minutes. What's more, you could turn to Cecily's uncle if anything went wrong. He has a house in the Hamptons."

Ellen said, her pulses quickening, "I know." After a moment she added, "Mr. Vandering's partner also has a place out there, hasn't he?"

Janet Vandering's suddenly distant tone told Ellen what she thought of her ex-husband's Red Hook-born partner. "Yes. I've heard it is quite an elaborate beach house. I've never been there."

"When would you want me to take Cecily out to the Hamptons?"

"Next weekend. Mainwaring closes earlier than the pub-

122

lic schools."

"May I telephone you about this tonight? I'm almost certain the answer will be yes, but I'd like a few hours to think it over."

"Of course. I'll be home. And I never go to bed until eleven."

"One thing more. I wouldn't want to accept a salary. I'm fairly prosperous at the moment, thanks to TV residuals. It will be more than enough to have a place to stay out there."

"Just as you like." She stood up. "Then I'll hear from you tonight."

By ten that evening, Ellen had made her decision. There was an excellent chance that Cecily might break her silence, once she was away from the city where she had twice landed in Carson Clinic. And Ellen would enjoy the woods and farmlands and beaches of eastern Long Island enormously. True, she might miss some work. But she could arrange for her agent to phone her if some really lucrative job came along. Surely Mrs. Vandering wouldn't object to her leaving Cecily in the care of Martha Barlow for a few days.

She phoned Cecily's mother. Yes, Mrs. Vandering said, it would be perfectly all right if Ellen had to return to the city for a day or two. They arranged that Ellen should come to the Vandering apartment at nine on Saturday morning, and then hung up.

Minutes later, Ellen's phone rang. "How's my favorite actress?" Dan Reardon asked.

"Fine. How are you, and where?"

"Okay, and still on the banks of the Potomac."

"I read about your testimony before that Congressional

committee."

He sounded pleased and astonished. "Why, that was just a little item in the financial section of the *Times*."

"I know, but your name caught my eye, and I read it." According to the story, Dan had argued that Vandering pre-fabs offered good value for housing under twenty thousand dollars, since statistics showed that the average couple buying a low-cost house kept it only three to five years before moving on to something better. Thus a Vandering pre-fab might provide modest shelter to as many as five young families before the foundation crumbled and doors and windows became hopelessly warped, as Dan admitted they would. Ellen had been able to imagine the brash smile with which he admitted it.

"Is your testimony over?"

"Yes. I don't know what the committee will decide."

"What's keeping you down there? Bribery and corruption?"

"You might call it that. Nothing crude, you understand. Just a reminder here and there of past favors, and a hint of favors to come. But I'll be back in New York next weekend, so how about having dinnner with me?"

"I'll be out in the Hamptons," she said, and explained about her arrangement with Janet Vandering.

"So you haven't taken my advice about Cecily?"

"No."

"Well, I can't say I'm sorry to hear you'll be in the Hamptons. I spend as much time out there as I can during the summer."

"I should think you would."

"Well, see you. Weekend after next, probably. Good night, Ellen."

Miss Amanda Mainwaring moved down darkened Sixty-eighth Street with Cleo, her Labrador retriever, padding beside her. Even though the hour was close to midnight, and even though she knew elderly women were favorite targets of muggers, she walked without fear. Cleo, like all Labradors, was one of the gentlest creatures alive. But few people knew that. They took one look at the fangs and the hanging red tongue, at the shiny black body the size of a half-grown calf's, and moved to the far edge of the sidewalk.

Anyway, just in case a criminal knowledgeable about Labradors did come along, she carried a can of hair spray in her purse.

As always on these late-night walks, she stopped before the Mainwaring School and stared at its dark façade. That morning she had received a long-awaited phone call from Irene Jackson, the school's assistant housekeeper, whom Amanda herself had hired many years ago as a kitchen maid. She had finally managed to learn, Irene told her, that the Vandering child would enter some other school in the fall.

Miss Mainwaring had felt disappointed. She had hoped that when the girl was next found with drugs in her possession, as was inevitable, and when the whole thing finally came to the attention of the police, as was also inevitable, she would still be a pupil of the Mainwaring School. Even so, the situation was still good, from Amanda Mainwaring's point of view. The prospect of giving parents of other pupils a satisfactory explanation of why the Vandering name no longer ornamented the roster must be causing her niece some uneasy nights. And on the day when the inevitable newspaper photograph appeared—Cecily, moving with one or both of her distraught parents up the steps of the Criminal Courts Building—the accompanying story might very well mention that the child had been introduced to the use of heroin while a student of the Mainwaring School. Yes, all in all, things were going well.

With Cleo padding silently beside her, she moved up the street.

thirteen

Shortly before noon the next Saturday, a tall, thin man stepped into a public phone booth on Second Avenue, deposited a coin, and dialed. After a moment he said, "This is Joe."

The voice at the other end of the line said sharply, "I told you never to phone me."

"I know, but something's come up. Barney says he saw the kid driving away from her mother's apartment house this morning. That Swede couple was in the front seat, and that actress was in the back with the kid."

"And so?"

"Barney says they had a lot of luggage with them. Looks like they've gone away for the summer. I thought you ought to know."

"What makes you think I didn't know?"

"Well, I—"

"Anyway, you're not paid to think. You're paid to do what I tell you, when I tell you to."

Resentment came into Joe's voice. "That kid may talk, if she's alone for a long time with that actress. Just because a kid won't spill something to a parent don't mean—"

"Now listen to me. She hasn't talked so far, and that means she's afraid to. Anyway, who would believe her? They'd figure she was just trying to cover up for some classmate. And even if somebody did believe her enough to have her look at police photographs, she wouldn't find a picture of either of you two. All you have to worry about is getting caught red-handed the next time you contact her, and that won't happen as long as I do your thinking for you."

"You planning to wait until they come back before—"

"No! I'll give you your orders when the time comes. Now don't phone me again."

"Okay, okay." Joe hung up.

When the station wagon emerged from the narrow private road that led through the woods, Ellen saw with relief that the house, a white colonial set far back on a wide lawn, was quite large—large enough that she would be able to isolate herself from Martha Barlow except at mealtimes.

Within minutes after the station wagon picked up Martha Barlow at her apartment house far out in Queens, Ellen had begun to dislike her. For one thing, there was her rudeness to Cecily. When the child asked why she wasn't wearing her diamond ring, Martha Barlow replied, "If you have to know, Miss Nosey, it's being cleaned." After that she launched upon a series of complaints. About her three cats, whom she'd had to leave behind, just as she did whenever she stayed at the Vandering apartment, because her cousin feared they would claw the furniture. About what the Long Island dampness would do to her rheumatism. About the isolation of the house, which would mean that if she wanted to do personal shopping she would have to ask Lindquist or somebody to drive her, since she herself didn't drive.

At last Ellen couldn't resist saying, "You should have mentioned all this to Mrs. Vandering. I'm sure she wouldn't have insisted on your going out there."

Martha Barlow said grudgingly, "Well, I figure it's better than being stuck in the city all summer."

"Most anyone would. I'm sure Mrs. Vandering could have rented out her house for five thousand or more. Personally, I think you and I are lucky."

The look the woman sent her from under wrinkled eyelids was so baleful that Ellen felt chilled. There must not be open enmity between her and Martha Barlow. It would be an unpleasant way to live for three months. More importantly, it would make impossible the relaxed, healing atmosphere she wanted to create for the young emotional casualty who sat between them.

She said, "But I do realize how you'll miss your cats. I'd certainly keep a cat if my landlord allowed tenants to have pets. It's too bad you couldn't bring yours with you."

Martha shrugged. "Beggars can't be choosers." But she sounded mollified.

Now, with the luggage-laden Lindquist moving tall and heavy-shouldered ahead of them, they climbed the broad white steps. Lindquist set down some of his burden to unlock the door, and then stood aside. Ellen stepped into the house, noticing as she did so the huge Chinese vases, set on teakwood stands, which stood just inside the threshold flanking the doorway.

Since the house had been shut up all winter, Ellen had expected to find it musty. Instead the air in the gleaming-

129

floored hall was fresh and delicately scented with lemon oil polish. In answer to her comment, Mrs. Lindquist explained that Mrs. Vandering always hired a local firm to clean and air the house before she came out to it.

"Did she tell you which rooms we were to have?"

"She left it up to me. I thought that you and Miss Cecily might like rooms near each other in the west wing. I'll put Mrs. Barlow in the other wing. Better for her rheumatism, since she'll be a few feet farther from the bay."

So Mrs. Lindquist had heard the conversation in the back seat. Was she being satirical now? The broad Scandinavian face offered no clue. But anyway, Ellen was grateful for the arrangement.

She had just finished unpacking in her airy, chintz-hung room when she heard a telephone ring. Going out into the hall, she saw a phone on a mahogany table. She lifted it from its cradle and said hello.

"I thought you'd be there by now," Len Vandering said. "Welcome to the Hamptons."

"Thank you."

"Has Niobe been weeping for her cats?" She had told him two nights before in New York that Mrs. Vandering's cousin was also to occupy the Long Island house.

"Len!"

"I know. Extension phones all over the place. Anyway, I moved out here yesterday, bag, baggage, and easel. I realize you'll want time to get settled. But how about my picking you up around seven tomorrow night for dinner?"

"Love it."

"Fine. See you then."

She moved on down the hall to the open door of the room where she had left Cecily unpacking a suitcase.

130

Glancing inside, she saw that the room was empty. With a vague sense of alarm, she hurried down the stairs.

Mrs. Barlow stood in the lower hall, staring at an oil painting Ellen had not noticed when she entered the house —a portrait of Janet Vandering seated on a Victorian sofa, with her dark-haired daughter, aged about three, leaning against her knee. Seeing the woman's tight lips and narrowed eyes as she gazed at the portrait, Ellen realized that Mrs. Barlow felt more than an understandable envy of her rich, beautiful cousin. She loathed her.

"Mrs. Barlow, have you seen Cecily?"

The woman turned her head. Perhaps she didn't realize how revealing her face had been. Or perhaps she didn't care. Anyway, her manner was unembarrassed. "You mean she isn't in her room? No, I didn't see her. Maybe she went out the back way."

Ellen's sense of alarm increased. That morning in the Vandering apartment, while Cecily was still in her room, Ellen and Mrs. Vandering had agreed that the child shouldn't be allowed to wander about alone. Turning, Ellen hurried back along the hall, and then paused beside the open doorway of a big kitchen. Lindquist was placing canned goods on a cupboard shelf. His wife stood beside the sink, shelling peas into a colander.

"Have either of you seen Cecily?"

Mrs. Lindquist said, "I saw her go out the back door about ten minutes ago. Lunch at two all right with you, Miss Stacey?"

"Of course. Do you have any idea where she might have gone?"

"Try the beach. If you go to the west side of the house, you'll see the path through the trees."

Going out the back door, Ellen moved around the house to the west lawn. Yes, there was the opening in the trees. She hurried along the path, too uneasy to be more than vaguely aware of bird song and the tender green of newly unfurled leaves, translucent in the sunlight. She turned a bend in the path, and then stopped short. Cecily stood a few feet away among the trees, staring down.

"Cecily!"

The small white face which turned toward her looked so drawn, so unchildlike, that Ellen cried, "What is it?" and hurried to her side.

"Nothing." Her voice was dull. "A long time ago there used to be a pool here, that's all."

Ellen looked down at a slight depression in the earth, filled with long grass and with small pink wildflowers whose name she didn't know. "What happened to the pool?"

"It just dried up, I guess. One year it was beautiful. Daddy and I found it. But when Mother and I came back the next year, it was just a brown puddle."

Ellen waited, with an odd sense that the child had revealed something about her closely guarded inner life, if only one could interpret it. But when the silence lengthened, Ellen said, "Well, it's pretty now, with the grass and the little flowers."

"Yes. You want to see the beach?"

Emerging from the trees less than a minute later, Ellen saw that it wasn't much of a beach. Just a stretch of sand about fifteen feet wide, strewn with pebbles. Beyond it lay the calm blue waters of the bay.

They sat down side by side on the sand. After a while Ellen said cautiously, "What happened to the pool still bothers you, doesn't it?"

No answer for several seconds. Then, with a rush: "It didn't just happen to the pool. It happened to me, too."

Easy, Ellen told herself, take it easy. "What do you mean?"

"It's a feeling I get, a brown-puddle feeling. When I saw it, after the divorce, I felt I was like that, all muddy and—and—"

"Bad?"

The dark head nodded.

Ellen made her voice matter of fact. "And you thought that was why your father had moved away from you and your mother? Because you'd somehow turned muddy and bad?"

The answer was low. "Yes."

So what Ellen had heard was true. Divorced parents, even intelligent ones like Howard and Janet Vandering, sometimes unknowingly inflicted upon a child a terrible secret burden, a conviction of having been to blame for the shattered marriage. Throat aching, Ellen waited until she was sure she would sound calm.

"I can see how you might feel that way at—six, wasn't it? But you're eleven now. And you still have that bad feeling about yourself?"

Cecily stared out over the bay. "Yes."

Ellen said in a casual tone, "You're really quite a conceited girl, aren't you?"

The face that swung toward her held hurt astonishment. "Conceited?"

"What would you call it? Apparently you thought you were all that mattered in your parents' marriage. And so when it broke up, you were sure it was because of you." She paused. "Didn't they give you any reason for the divorce?"

Confusion had come into Cecily's face. "I think—I think they said that they didn't get along. But that doesn't seem much of a reason."

No, Ellen admitted silently, it certainly wouldn't have seemed enough of a reason, not to a heartbroken child.

Cecily went on in a small voice, "You mean there really could have been some reason besides me, some reason so important that they—"

"That they felt they couldn't go on together? Yes."

"What sort of reason?"

Ellen thought for a moment, and then grimly decided to take the plunge. Janet Vandering might feel outraged, if she ever heard about it. Certainly Ellen's own mother would be horrified by the very idea. But the important consideration was the child. Somehow she had to be jolted out of her sense of guilt and unworthiness.

"Cecily, don't they teach you anything about men and women at that school of yours?"

"You mean sex education?" Her voice was puzzled. "Oh, yes. We had that."

"Well, sometimes married couples find they are no longer attracted to each other. And sometimes when that happens, although not always, they get a divorce. I'm not saying that's what happened to your mother and father, but it could have been."

Again Cecily stared out over the bay. Ellen waited tensely. Had she made a mistake? Had she just added a new element to the child's emotional turmoil?

Cecily turned to her. "Then maybe it didn't have a thing to do with me?"

For the first time, Ellen saw actual eagerness in the

gray eyes. She expelled her pent-up breath and then said, smiling, "Of course it didn't. Both your parents loved you from the day you were born, and they still do. That's something that almost never changes."

Cecily's eyes searched Ellen's face for several seconds. Then she burst out, "But if there isn't something wrong with me, why did those two men—" She broke off.

"What two men?"

Cecily's voice was feverish. "You won't tell?"

"Darling, I can't promise, not until I know what it is. But this I can promise you. You won't come to any harm through anything you tell me."

For a moment Ellen saw conflict in the upturned face. Then Cecily said, "I want to tell you. I've wanted to for a long time. It—it happened the day Miss Beazley took us to the aquarium."

She told about all three times. The time at the aquarium. And the time on the path leading to the Alice statue. And the last time, when there'd been only one of them, the stocky one, with a tool kit in his hand, and she had caught the bus that took her up to the Cloisters, and gone into the ladies' room and sniffed the powder. . . .

Ellen listened with a sense of shock strongly modified by disbelief. At last she said, "Are you sure this happened? On three different occasions these men walked up to you and gave you heroin?"

"Yes, only once it was just the short one."

"You told your parents you found it under a bush."

"Yes, but it wasn't true."

"You're sure you didn't get it from some girl at your school?"

"No! Mother and Daddy think that, but it isn't so."

"Now these two men. Have you ever seen either of them before that day in the aquarium?"

Cecily shook her head. "You won't tell anyone, will you? They said they'd—find me if I told. They might even come out here, and I don't want to ever see them again. So you won't tell, will you?"

Ellen said slowly, "I don't know." Perhaps she had no right to keep it from the Vanderings. On the other hand, she hated to add to their distress over Cecily's drug-taking by revealing to them just how accomplished a fantasist their child was. "Let's leave it this way. If I do decide to tell anyone, I'll talk it over with you first. Is that fair?"

After a moment Cecily said in a serious voice, "Yes, that's fair."

Ellen glanced at her watch. "Come on! We're late for lunch."

As they moved up the path through the trees, Ellen wondered if the child might be even more disturbed than anyone had realized. If she were given, not just to fantasy, but to actual hallucinations . . . But probably, Ellen thought, with a wry inward smile, she was just an incipient writer of TV melodramas. The whole thing sounded like a variation of some episode she might have seen on TV. The two mysterious strangers, one tall, one shorter and carrying a tool kit . . .

A tool kit.

As one tends to do with unpleasant matters, Ellen had thrust to the back of her mind the memory of her near-plunge to the first floor of that old movie theater. But now she recalled the sound of hammers, the smell of blowtorch-heated metal, the tool-laden workmen, one or two of whom might not have been workmen at all. . . .

Just think about it for a moment, she told herself, vaguely aware of a brown thrasher, a twig in its long beak, who flew across the path. What if the child moving ahead of her through the leaf-dappled sunlight had told the truth?

After all, even in her semiconscious state that day at the Cloisters, she had referred to a "they" who supplied her with heroin. What if the adults around her, including Ellen herself, had been too hasty in dismissing that as either an outright lie or a drug-induced fantasy? What if the two men really existed?

If they did, obviously they were hirelings. No professional pusher would give away valuable drugs in such quantities. Ruling out Cecily's parents, which of the people around her could have done such a hideous thing as to pay someone to give drugs to a child?

Dan Reardon's toughly handsome face rose before her. Probably he had enough money to hire someone to do almost anything. Furthermore, at least some of the people he had grown up with in that tough neighborhood must have turned to the drug traffic. But what possible motive could he have to harm the daughter of his partner? Certainly he didn't seem to dislike Howard Vandering. At the very worst, he might feel a bit of amiable contempt for the older man's ineptitude.

Len Vandering? Despite an inward shrinking, she forced herself to consider Cecily's uncle. Even though he lived in a poor neighborhood, he obviously had a good income. What was more, a resident of the East Village could easily make contact with dealers in drugs. And at least in the past, he had bitterly resented his half-brother. But had he ever resented him *that* much? Ellen couldn't believe it, especially when she considered that Len seemed to feel affection for his niece, an affection that Cecily, withdrawn as she was, apparently returned.

No, it was impossible to think of Len wanting to harm Cecily because of some lingering jealousy of his brother. And what other motive could he possibly have?

As for Martha Barlow, she obviously hated her rich, pretty cousin, and perhaps might be glad of any sort of grief that came her way. But no criminal, however depraved, would carry out such a dangerous assignment unless assured of substantial payment. And, as far as anyone seemed to know, Martha had barely enough income to support herself and her cats.

Amanda Mainwaring, who had been walking past the school that afternoon. There had been the authentic glitter of madness in the old eyes in that patrician face as she spoke of her usurping niece. But no matter how mad, would an elderly woman of good background ever conceive of such a scheme to bring the school and her niece into disrepute, let alone know how to carry it out?

Who else, then? It seemed to Ellen that there was someone else she knew of, someone who harbored bitterness against one or both of the Vanderings, but the person's identity eluded her.

Forget it. Why distress herself over two men who almost certainly had no existence outside the imagination of a disturbed child?

They were crossing the lawn now. Ellen looked down at Cecily, and felt a thrill of surprised pleasure. Already the child's face had lost some of its remoteness. She moved differently, too, not with shoulders tense and head slightly lowered, but more easily, and with her gaze fixed on the house.

That talk about the divorce had done Cecily good—a world of good. As for her story about the two men—well, in a day or so Ellen would lead her to talk of them again, and when inconsistencies in her story arose, as they undoubtedly would, Ellen would point them out to her. Eventually, the child might abandon the story entirely, and tell the truth.

Ellen said, "We'd better go straight upstairs and get ready for lunch."

"I hope it's a big lunch." Her voice, too, was different, holding a new vibrancy. "I'm starved."

When they entered the house, Martha was coming down the stairs. She said, continuing her descent, "Lunch was supposed to be at two. You're late."

Moving past her up the stairs, Cecily said over her shoulder, "And am I ever hungry!"

Martha stared after the small figure until she reached the landing. Then she said, descending to the hall, "What's got into her? I never saw her so lively."

"Maybe it's the good clean air." Unable to conceal her hope, her sense of accomplishment, she added, "I think she's going to be all right."

Martha stared at her. "That one? Never. She'll be dead before she's twenty-five."

Ellen felt a surge of anger. "How can you say that?"

"Once they get started that way—"

"On drugs?" Ellen had gotten her voice under control. "Cecily isn't an addict."

"Just wait until she's a little older. Unless she's locked up somewhere, nobody will be able to watch her all the time. And statistics show," she said, in that dogmatic tone with which people quote statistics, "that the average addict lives only ten to fifteen years after he starts. No, Cecily will never inherit her father's money."

The Vandering money. That was something she had not thought of as she moved up the path from the beach, considering the possible motives someone might have to harm Cecily.

Reluctant to discuss such matters with Martha, and yet feeling a need to know, she asked, "In that case, who would inherit?"

"Not Janet." The words conveyed grim relish. "She gave up all claim to Howard's estate when she got that fat divorce settlement." She paused and then said, "I suppose the next person in line is his half-brother, that crazy artist."

Ellen's stomach tightened. "Yes, I suppose he would have to be," she said, and started up the stairs.

A little before ten that night, Cecily stood beside the darkened window of her room, staring out over the moonlit lawn to the wall of trees beyond. Until a few minutes ago, this had been the best day of her life, or at least the best in years and years. First, Ellen had gotten her over that dumb, little-kid idea about the divorce. It was such a little-kid idea that Cecily felt ashamed of having had it so long. And Ellen was right. It had been conceited of her, as well as dumb, to ever think that *she* was the cause, instead of something to do with that love-and-sex business that grownups seemed to make such a fuss about.

And it had felt good to tell Ellen about the two men, after thinking about them all by herself for so long. True, Ellen hadn't said what she thought about them, but they could talk that over later.

After lunch, she and Ellen had spent the rest of the day

on the beach. Neither of them had mentioned the two men. Instead they had talked about all sorts of things, like the way scallops, in the fall, swam in that crazy, flip-flopping way through the shallow water, and whether Fagin in *Oliver!* was more funny than scary or the other way around, and if your sunburn starts to peel, should you leave it alone or peel it off yourself.

Mrs. Lindquist had made a good dinner. Afterwards Cousin Martha had gone to her room, which was nice, leaving the two of them to watch a TV show about whales. At nine-thirty, feeling sunburned and sleepy, Cecily had gone up to her room.

She had been almost asleep when she heard Ellen pass by in the hall. She knew it was Ellen, first because Cousin Martha was in the other wing and the Lindquists in their own apartment over the garage, and second because the step was so light, lighter even than her mother's, and much lighter than Amy's had been. . . .

Amy.

She had sat bolt upright in bed then, staring at the window, a blue-white rectangle of moonlight.

In the ladies' room at the Palm Court that afternoon, Ellen had told her that the police said thieves had killed Amy, and that it must be true, because the police knew about such things. Cecily had wanted to believe that. In fact, ever since that day at the Plaza she had tried not to think about Amy at all. This afternoon, for instance, she had skipped all mention of Amy when she told Ellen about the two men.

But Amy had been there that day, at the foot of the path leading toward the Alice statue. And that night she had died. What if the police were wrong about why she

141

had died? What if, after all, it had been those two men who had killed her, because they were afraid she might guess what it was the tall one had put in Cecily's pocket?

But if they had done that to Amy, just because she might have guessed, what might they do to Ellen? Ellen, who knew, because Cecily herself had told her.

Cold with fear, she had thrown back the blankets and crossed to the window. Surely there must be some way of taking back what she had told. Now, as she stood there, the answer came to her. She had been able to tell that Ellen was doubtful about the two men. Probably Ellen really believed, as Cecily's parents did, that she had got those packets from some other girl at school.

Why not say it was another girl?

But what girl? They would want her to name someone, and if she did, her parents and the whole school would come down on the girl, and she would deny it. Cecily would have to name some girl who was no longer at the school. The Greek girl, Christina? No, Christina was at a school in Connecticut, where she could be reached.

Amala Chardis! She could be the one. Amala, who would never be bothered, who would never even know about it, because she was thousands of miles away now, and not coming back.

She waited until she had the story straight in her head. Then she picked up her pink quilted robe from a chairback, slipped into it, and walked down the hall.

When she heard the light tap on her door, Ellen placed the book she had been trying to read, without too much success, on the stand beside her bed. She, too, had enjoyed the hours of sand and sea and sun today. And she'd had the added joy of watching the new animation in Cecily's face. But always at the back of her mind there had been the child's story, and the thought of Len Vandering, next in line for all that money. . . .

"Come in," she said, and then, as the door opened: "Can't sleep?" She patted the edge of the bed. "Sit down. Good heavens, no slippers. I'll move over so you can curl your feet up under your robe."

When she was settled on the edge of the bed, Cecily said, with a rush, "Ellen, I made up all that about those two men."

Until now, when she felt a vast relief, Ellen had not realized just how heavily the child's story had weighed upon her. "You did?" She kept her voice calm. "I rather thought you had."

"You see, I—I got that stuff from a girl at school."

"Care to tell me about it?"

"Her name was Amala Chardis."

"What an odd name. It sounds foreign."

Cecily nodded. "I forget which country she was from, but her father was with the U.N."

"Was?"

"His government gave him another job, right after Easter vacation. A better one, Amala said. They were all going home first, and then her father was going to be ambassador to Brazil, or some country like that."

"Perhaps that is a better job." She paused, and then asked casually, "Did Amala tell you how she got the drug?"

"Yes. She used to snitch it from her brother. He was grown-up, almost twenty."

"And Amala won't be back to school next year?"

"No, I guess she's gone for good."

"Cecily, why did you wait until now to tell me this?"

143

The answer was prompt. "You see, if you tell on a girl, you're a ratfink, and I didn't want to be one. But tonight I got to thinking, and I decided that since Amala was gone, it wouldn't make me a ratfink to tell."

Ellen studied her. The child's explanation had been a little too glib to ring true. Perhaps there was some other girl besides Amala who . . .

"I think that's a sensible way to look at it. But, Cecily, what if another girl, or anybody, offers you drugs?"

Her voice held unmistakable fervor. "I won't use it I—I won't need to, now."

Ellen smiled. I wouldn't trade this moment, she thought, for the lead in Neil Simon's next play.

"Then you'd better go to bed now. We have a busy day ahead of us, what with swimming and working on our tans."

As Cecily walked back down the hall, she felt so at peace that drowsiness had begun to creep over her again. It was all right now. Those men would never know she had told Ellen.

Maybe she could pretend for the rest of the summer that they weren't real. They wouldn't come out here. They were city men. And in the fall—well, if they showed up someplace, and gave her something, she would just wait until she was alone, and throw it away.

In the living room of the comfortable apartment above the garage, Elsa Lindquist looked up from her copy of the *National Enquirer* and asked, "You get things fixed up with that butcher today?"

Thor Lindquist, eyes still fixed on the TV screen where two middleweights pummeled each other in a dispirited fashion, laid his pipe down in a crystal ashtray which, until a few weeks before, had rested on one of the small tables in Janet Vandering's apartment. When he got around to it, he would take it to a Southampton shop which bought crystalware. In the meantime, he might as well use it.

"Yes. I couldn't get him to go to fifteen. We settled for twelve percent, six for him and six for me."

Mrs. Lindquist snorted. "He could add twenty percent to the bills, and she'd never know the difference."

"Reminds me. The butcher told me how one summer he found he'd messed up his accounts, sent some customer a crown rib roast without charging for it. So he sent bills to fourteen customers who often ordered crown ribs, figuring the right one would pay for it and the others tell him it was a mistake. All fourteen paid without a peep out of them." He shook his head. "Rich people!"

"Well, I hope that Miss Stacey doesn't get a look at the bills. She isn't rich. And she impresses me as pretty smart."

"Oh, I don't think we need to worry about her in any way," her husband said, and reached for his pipe.

fourteen

Shortly after seven the next evening, a red Austin Healey carried Len and Ellen along a winding asphalt highway bordered by oaks and maples. In the near-sunset light, tree trunks had taken on a pinkish cast, and newly opened oak leaves, still more gray than green, had turned a dull bronze.

Ellen said, "I hate to tell you this, but I'd like to be home by ten o'clock."

"Ten o'clock! That's practically the middle of the afternoon."

"I know. But today Cecily mentioned that she'd never seen dawn, and I was silly enough to promise that tomorrow we'd both get up and see it. Dawn comes early in June."

"That it does. Well, I suppose a promise is a promise. Incidentally, what's happened to her? Tonight she seemed—well, almost like a normal child."

"I think she will be." Her voice held pride. "Len, she opened up to me! She told me a lot of things, including where she got the heroin."

His startled face swung toward her. After a moment he said, eyes again fixed on the road, "Good going. Where did she get it?"

"From a classmate." She repeated Cecily's story about Amala Chardis.

"Do Howard and Janet know yet?"

"Yes. At least I called her father this morning. He seemed terribly relieved. He's going to check, but he's certain the girl is out of the school and out of the country. He remembers reading that a U.N. representative named Chardis was recalled over a month ago."

"How on earth did you get the little sphinx to talk?"

Ellen laughed. "Oh, I didn't get the truth right away. First she spun me a story about two men who'd kept giving her the stuff."

The car swerved momentarily over the white line, and then returned to its own lane. "Damn fool squirrel," Len said.

"I didn't see it."

"Well, he almost got himself killed. Now what's this about two men?"

She told him.

"Too much TV?" Len suggested.

"I imagine so. But also I gather that she's had a real conflict, poor mite. Since she likes me, she wanted to make me feel she was confiding in me, but at the same time she didn't want to tattle on a classmate. Hence the story she told me down at the beach. It took her almost eight hours, apparently, to decide that telling on a girl who had left the country wouldn't make her a ratfink, as she put it."

He shook his head. "Kids! And generation after generation they're told that childhood is the happiest time of their lives."

"Personally, I like being grown-up."

He grinned at her. "So do I, so do I."

By the time Len brought her home, the radiance of a full moon bathed the Vandering lawn. Ellen's pleasant memories of two hours at a Watermill restaurant—succulent steak, and a combo that played crisp, 'fifties-style jazz—was tinged with regret that, because of her promise to Cecily, the evening had to end so soon.

When he had stopped the car at the foot of the steps, Len said, "Please don't go in just yet. I want to talk to you." He reached over and took her hand. "It's about Dan Reardon. He has a place here in the Hamptons."

"I know."

"He'll be out here a lot, but I hope you won't see much of him." He went on swiftly, "It isn't just that I'm jealous, although of course I am. I can see how he might attract women. But he's not for someone like you."

Ellen scarcely heard the last sentence. Her attention had been caught by that arresting—and disturbing—"jealous." Then she gave herself a mental shake. Already she'd decided that she mustn't, just mustn't, fall in love with him. The most it could lead to would be an invitation to share his East Village apartment, where she would chat with his hippie neighbors, learn just how he liked his martinis, cook pleasant little dinners for him—and probably learn to like it so much that when the half-year, or year, or however long it lasted, was over, she would be utterly shattered. At twenty, broken hearts and crushed self-esteem usually could restore themselves. Nearing thirty, both hearts and egos became less elastic.

She asked lightly, "What have you got against him, except that he would never have made Skull and Bones?"

"There are stories about him. For instance, he's supposed to have, or have had in the past, heavy interests in

148

Las Vegas. You know what that means."

"Underworld connections? The Syndicate? But don't they often say that about successful men who've risen from his sort of background?"

"Yes, and most of the time it isn't true. But sometimes it is."

"Your brother surely doesn't believe those rumors. Otherwise he wouldn't have wanted Dan as a partner."

Len said wryly, "Poor Howard! He's determined to prove that Vandering financial genius didn't die with old Sam Vandering. I think he might turn to almost anyone who would help him prove it."

He paused and then added, smiling, "Well, if I can't warn you off Reardon, maybe the only thing to do is to keep you so busy you won't have time for him." His arm, encircling her shoulders, drew her close.

"Yes," she said, "that might work."

When she entered the house about ten minutes later, she looked through the open door of the small den across from the living room. Martha sat there watching an old movie on TV. She took her gaze from George Brent long enough to glance at Ellen. "You're home early."

"I promised Cecily to get up in time for dawn, remember."

"Catch *me*," Martha said, and returned her attention to George Brent, who had been joined by Bette Davis.

Up in her room, Ellen laid her handbag on the bureau and then turned out the light. Moving to the window, she looked at the moon-flooded front lawn and the curving wall of trees which encircled it. She felt keyed-up, and as wide awake as if the hour were noon. Maybe Len, she thought wryly, was the one she should stay away from.

149

A swim might relax her for sleep. And the quiet waters of the bay, after fourteen hours of June sunlight, would still be pleasantly warm. She turned on the light and began to undress.

When she descended the stairs a few minutes later, a white terry cloth robe over her bathing suit, Martha still sat before the TV set. "I'm going for a swim," Ellen explained.

"This time of night?" Without waiting for an answer, Martha turned her gaze to Bette Davis, who was wrangling in a genteel fashion with Geraldine Fitzgerald.

Enough bright moonlight filtered through the trees to make the path clearly visible. Ellen passed the spot where, the day before, Cecily had stood in silent mourning for a vanished pool, and then walked on toward the white gleam of sand.

She was halfway across the narrow beach and had stopped to untie the sash of her robe, when she became aware of a man who moved slowly and unsteadily toward her along the water's edge, his head lowered. She said, startled, "Who are you?"

Apparently he, too, was startled. Raising his head, he stopped short. She recognized the red hair, the thin face. Dale Haylock. At the same moment, she realized that Janet Vandering's angry suitor was the person whose identity had eluded her when, the day before, she had mentally reviewed those who might have a grudge against one or both of the Vanderings.

He said belligerently, moving closer, "The name's Haylock." She caught the aroma of gin. "And I might ask the same of you."

"Ellen Stacey. I'm afraid, Mr. Haylock, that I must ask what you're doing here."

"Ask away. It's none of your damned business."

Ellen said sharply, "But it is. Mrs. Vandering has turned her property over to me for the summer. People wandering around on her private beach are very much my business."

He scowled at her. "Look here, Miss Whoever-you-are. I'll bet I've known Janet a lot longer than you have. And better." His tone became brooding. "Three summers ago, she and I used to lie on this beach day after day. And we'd come down here on nights like this, too."

"I'm sorry." Her voice was more gentle. "How did you get here?"

"Drove." He sounded merely sullen now. "My car's up there on the private road."

"Well, please forgive me, but I don't think Mrs. Vandering would like your being here."

"Oh, hell! It was a lousy idea to come here anyway." Gait even more uneven in the softer sand, he crossed the beach and plunged into the trees at a point a few yards to the right of the path's entrance. She heard his thrashing progress through the underbrush, and then the sound of a car starting. As the hum of its engine dwindled, she slipped out of her robe.

Within a minute, she had forgotten him. Delighting in the water's silky caress, she swam out about twenty yards, then turned on her back and floated, rocked gently by the current. Above her the inverted bowl of the sky was so bright with moonlight that even major stars looked pale. When she began to feel chilled, she swam ashore and walked gingerly over the pebble-strewn sand to where she had left her robe and beach sandals.

It was then that she saw the dark figure, standing just at the edge of the woods.

For a moment, thinking he was Dale Haylock, she felt a rush of annoyance. Then uneasiness mingled with her irritation. It wasn't Dale Haylock. Some other man stood there in the trees' shadow. Someone an inch or so shorter, and heavier-set.

"You're beautiful," Dan Reardon said.

The huskiness of his voice, more than the words themselves, told her what he was feeling. Aware of her own instinctive female response to his admiration, she said, half pleased, half embarrassed, "Dan! You startled me. I couldn't see who you were." Bending, she picked up her robe.

"I'm sorry." He moved toward her. "I thought you'd recognize me, but I guess I was standing in shadow there."

She said, slipping into the robe he held for her, "I thought you were going to be in New York this weekend."

"I planned to, but then I changed my mind."

"When did you get out here?"

"To my beach place? Late yesterday. About an hour ago I decided to take a drive, and all of a sudden I thought, 'I'll see if Ellen's home.' When I got here, that cousin of Mrs. Vandering's told me you'd gone for a swim."

"Well, now that you're here, how about a drink?"

"Great."

As they crossed the beach toward the path, she said, "I'm afraid it will have to be a fairly quick drink, because I have to get up at four."

"Why? So you can kneel on your prayer rug, facing east?"

She laughed and explained about her promise to Cecily. When they emerged onto the lawn, Ellen saw the impressive town car standing in the circular drive. "A Rolls-Royce?"

"A Bentley. I planned to buy a Rolls, but somebody convinced me that would look ostentatious at this stage of the game."

"I pity the successful. The things they have to worry about!"

"Yeah. All you can say for it is that it's a hell of a lot better than failure."

Martha, they found, had apparently gone to bed, leaving the wall lights on in the hall. Ellen switched on a lamp in the living room. "Nice," Dan commented, looking around at the wide fireplace, the hooked rugs scattered about on the gleaming floor, the expensively casual furniture covered in heavy flowered linen.

"You've never been here before?"

"No, I didn't know Howard when this was his place, too."

"Well, that's a liquor cabinet over there in the corner. When I checked it yesterday, it seemed well-stocked. While I'm changing, pour yourself whatever you like."

"How about you?"

"A little brandy, please."

When she returned to the living room, wearing a skirt and top of pink cotton knit, she and Dan sat on one of the slip-covered sofas, she with a snifter of brandy and he with a Scotch and water. He said, "Congratulations. I hear you got Cecily to tell who her pusher was."

"How did you know?"

"As soon as I got to New York yesterday afternoon, I saw Howard. He's so damned relieved that the other kid, this Emilia—"

"Amala."

"Anyway, that she's left the country."

"Yes. He did sound pleased when I phoned him. He said it made up for everything else—business problems, I suppose he meant."

"He has them, all right. He'll either have to shore up that small airline of his with more money, or sell at a big loss. The trouble is I can't handle everything, and Howard can't put personal worries out of his mind and concentrate on business."

"Maybe he shouldn't have gone into business."

"He certainly shouldn't have. I often wonder why he hasn't gone into politics, like those other fellows who have inherited a few dozen million."

Minutes later he set down his empty glass. "Well," he said, standing, "I'd better leave, since you have to wake up at dawn. Besides, we'd better get an early start back to the city tomorrow."

"We?"

He looked a little embarrassed. "I have a weekend guest."

She asked, as they moved toward the hall, "Someone like Delphine?"

"As a matter of fact, it is Delphine. Since I knew you wouldn't be in New York, I called her up. Halfway through dinner last night we decided to drive out to the Hamptons."

Ellen wondered, but didn't ask, what Delphine was doing while her host played a surprise call on another lady.

She said good night to him at the door, and then went up to her room, pausing on the way to look in at the slumbering Cecily. Dan Reardon was a strange man, she thought, as she slipped a nightgown over her head. Even before that moment on the beach, she had been aware that he not only liked her, but felt strongly attracted to her. And yet he'd

154

never even tried to hold her hand.

Glancing at her small alarm clock, she saw with dismay that its hands pointed to ten of twelve. Oh, well, she thought, as she set the alarm for four o'clock, maybe she could get a nap tomorrow afternoon.

fifteen

It was in a specialty shop on Southampton's Job's Lane that, two days later, Ellen again met Dan's friend Delphine. With Martha Barlow and Cecily, Ellen was about to leave the shop when a tall brunette wearing a white pantsuit and oversized dark glasses approached.

"Say, don't I know you? Weren't you having lunch with Dan Reardon one day in town when I stopped at your table?"

"I remember."

"Could I speak to you for a minute?"

Something in the girl's manner made Ellen think that whatever she had to say might not be for Cecily's ears. Turning to Martha, she suggested, "Why don't you two wait for me in the car?"

Frustrated curiosity in her little gray eyes, Martha said, "Oh, all right. Come on, Cecily."

When the shop door had closed behind the woman and child, Delphine said, "Over here," and led Ellen to a corner hidden from most of the rest of the shop by a rack of dresses.

"Look," the brunette said, "I can tell Dan thinks a lot of

you from the way he acted when I asked him about you. Not that he'd say much. He wouldn't even tell me your name."

"How do you do," the brunette said primly. "I'm Delphine Carter. Anyway, Dan said you were a nice girl, and so I figure you ought to know what kind of a guy he is."

She took off the dark glasses. With dismay, Ellen looked at her swollen and empurpled left eye. "You mean that Dan—?"

"Sure. Last Sunday night." She replaced the glasses.

Feeling a little sick, Ellen said, "It's hard to believe—"

"Sure it's hard—for you. He probably treats you like you were made of spun glass."

"But that's awful! Why on earth should he—?"

"It's Stacey—Ellen Stacey."

"We drove out to that fancy beach house of his Saturday night, see. Sunday night he got restless and went for a drive. Not with that houseman of his who sometimes drives him around, but alone. He didn't even ask me to go. When he came back, we had a little argument, and he belted me one and then threw me out."

"Threw you out!"

"He gave me fifty dollars for a hotel room and train fare to New York, and then told the houseman to drive me into Southampton. Some girls I know have rented a house here for the summer, so I decided to save the fifty. I had him drop me at my friends' house."

"I'm sorry; terribly sorry."

"I just thought you ought to know, that's all. Say, look at this." She took a long evening dress of green silk jersey from the rack and held it against her. "How would this look on me?"

157

"Marvelous," Ellen said feebly, edging toward the door. "Well, good-by."

" 'By. If you see Dan, tell him I hope he gets leprosy."

Out on the sidewalk, Ellen moved slowly toward the parked station wagon. Despite Dan's reputation for rough business tactics, she had liked him. But sharp business practices were one thing. Blacking the eye of a hundred-and-ten-pound girl was another.

Of course, Delphine could have been lying as to how she acquired that black eye. But Ellen didn't think she had been. Nor could she conceive of any behavior on Delphine's part outrageous enough to have justified Dan's action.

Forcing her lips into a smile, she moved to the station wagon and opened the door on the driver's side.

The next two weeks were the most pleasant Ellen had known for years. Except for two days spent in New York making a hair conditioner commercial, she swam each morning from the pebble-strewn beach. With Len Vandering and Cecily, she skimmed over Peconic Bay in a rented catboat. Sometimes with both of them, sometimes just with Len, she rode in the Austin Healey through farmlands and small villages, now lapped by the green tide of full summer. Her blond hair became sun-streaked, and she and her young charge acquired deep tans and ravenous appetites.

Twice in the afternoon Len drove her and Cecily over to his small beach house, set on stilts on a point of land curving into the bay. The second time they were there, he asked if they would mind his taking "five minutes" to put the finishing touches on a picture. For over an hour, while Cecily basked on the sundeck, Ellen watched him at his easel beside the cluttered worktable, painting with such concentration that she felt he'd forgotten his guests as well as the time.

Cecily's parents phoned frequently—her mother from Cape Cod and her father from New York, and talked to both their daughter and Ellen. During a phone conversation about ten days after Ellen had repeated to him Cecily's story about Amala Chardis, Howard Vandering said, "If only I could express what a difference it's made in my life, knowing who the child was, and that she's out of the country. I won't go into details, Miss Stacey, but until now I've shoved far too much of the workload onto Dan Reardon's shoulders. Now I'm really beginning to take hold myself."

"I'm glad."

"You seeing much of that young brother of mine?"

"Quite a lot."

"Good. Maybe you'll keep him as well as my daughter out of mischief."

In fact, she was seeing Len almost every day. If part of his purpose was, as he had jokingly said, to keep her so busy she would have no time for Dan Reardon, then his efforts were unnecessary. Dan hadn't shown up again, or even telephoned. Because of the memory of Delphine's empurpled eye, Ellen on the whole felt relieved not to hear from him.

Two afternoons after her phone conversation with Cecily's father, Ellen and Len were driving along a pine-bordered road near Amagansett when the car slowed. "The entrance to Reardon's place is just ahead. Want to drive in and take a look?"

"You mean, just drop in?"

"Probably he won't even be there. My brother tells me Reardon's been sticking pretty close to New York lately.

159

But we can look at the outside of the house."

"All right."

Seconds later they turned left onto a narrow road, past a sign which read, "Private Drive. No Trespassing." Len said, "Perhaps we'll get to see his yacht."

"I didn't know he had one. Is it big?"

"You might call it roomy. Passenger accommodations for twelve."

"I had no idea. He must be almost as rich as Onassis."

"Nowhere near. But give him time."

The road began to descend through an artificial cut, its sandy faces planted with soil-retaining evergreens. "There's his place."

On the beach below sat a white stucco house. Long and low and with a red tile roof, it looked like a transplanted bit of southern California. Beside a pier that stretched out into the bay, a graceful white yacht rode at anchor. Closer inshore, a small power boat was secured fore and aft by lines running from its deck to stanchions on the pier.

Len said, "Look, Dan is here, or at least his Bentley is." Through the raised door of the garage attached to the left side of the house, Ellen could see the expensive English car, as well as a small sports car and a gray station wagon.

She said, "Do you think we really ought to barge in on him?"

"Sure." He grinned at her. "It'll needle him, us showing up together."

"I thought men were supposed to be above malicious little tricks."

"Don't you believe it."

Leaving the car on the apron of asphalt behind the attached garage, they walked toward the front of the house.

160

Now Ellen could see a man in a bos'n's chair, painting the yacht's raffish smokestack.

The façade of the house was almost entirely glass, screened by curtains of beige mesh. Len pushed the bell, and after a moment the door was opened by a slender man of about forty with an olive-skinned face.

"Hello, Emilio. Is Mr. Reardon in?"

"Yes, Mr. Vandering. Come in, please."

As Ellen and Len stepped into the living room—a long one, furnished in a blend of modern furniture and either fake or real Spanish antiques—Dan's voice, sounding surprised and irritated, called from another room, "That you, Howard?"

"Wrong Vandering," Len called back. When Dan, wearing dark slacks and a blue pullover, appeared in a doorway, Len added, "But I figured that even if you didn't want to see me, you'd be glad to see Ellen."

She couldn't tell whether or not he was glad. True, there was warmth in the dark blue eyes resting on her face. But she could also see, despite his efforts to hide it, that he felt annoyed, perhaps by Len's bland air of oneupmanship, perhaps just by receiving unexpected visitors.

She said, "Hello, Dan. We won't stay. We shouldn't have barged in on you like this."

"No, no. I'm glad to see you. It's just that I hope you won't mind sitting here in the den. I've got a dehumidifier going. My damned sinuses are acting up."

Ellen and Len followed him into a room that was much smaller—and in Ellen's opinion pleasanter—than the living room with its department store–decorator look. Here the chairs were of black leather, wall shelves held books—mostly concerned with finance, she noticed—and a window

161

gave a view up the driftwood-strewn beach stretching to a rocky headland.

When the houseman had brought them tall glasses of vodka and tonic, Len asked, "When did you get out here?"

"Yesterday. It was so hot in New York I couldn't stand it. And then when I got out here the damned dampness got to my sinuses. I ought to have built a place in the Adirondacks."

"You couldn't anchor that beautiful yacht in the Adirondacks," Ellen said.

"She is a nice-looking craft, isn't she? I'm sorry I can't take you aboard. I'm having her painted."

Len said, slapping his pockets, "Dan, have you got a cigarette?"

"Sorry. I gave up smoking two years ago. And Emilio doesn't smoke either." It was his turn to practice oneupmanship. "You ought to quit, too. All it takes is a little will power."

"Oh, I plan to quit, any year now. Will you both excuse me? I think I may have some cigarettes in the car."

When Len had gone, Dan smiled at her and said, "The Hamptons must agree with you. You look wonderful, Ellen."

"Thank you." She returned his smile. But now that she was alone with him, she had begun to think of Delphine's bruised and swollen eye.

"What have you and Cecily been up to?"

As she spoke of swimming, and sailing, and walking through the woods with binoculars and the bird book she and Cecily had found on a drugstore rack of paperbacks, she kept on thinking about Delphine. Was it in this room that he had swung his hard brown fist into the girl's fragile

162

face? The living room, a bedroom?

At last Dan said, "Sounds to me as if you're going to be the making of that kid." He paused. "Hey, I wonder what's keeping Len?"

"Probably there weren't any cigarettes in his car, and so he's driving around to find a place to buy them."

Dan shook his head. "Just like one of those shnooks in the anti-smoking commercials."

There was a brief silence. Then Ellen said, "Dan, do you remember that Sunday night you drove over to see me?"

"Of course I remember."

"Two days after that, I ran into Delphine Carter in a shop in Southampton."

The dark blue eyes became cool. "So?"

"She took off her sun glasses."

"And?"

"Her eye looked terrible. Dan, *did* you do that?"

"Give her a shiner? Damn right I did. Oh, I didn't mean to hurt her that much. I swung on her with my open hand, and she turned her head just then, and I caught her across the eye."

"But why? Why did you strike her?"

"I'll tell you why. When I got back, I caught her going through the bureau in my bedroom. I opened her purse, and there were some diamond cuff links I bought ten years ago. I don't wear them now. I decided they were too gaudy. But they're still damned valuable. And that greedy little broad, who I've always been generous with, was trying to steal them."

"All right. She was a thief. Why didn't you call the police?"

Dan said indignantly, "Why, I wouldn't do that to the

163

girl!" As Ellen stared at him, bewildered, he went on, "Believe you me, Delphine would a lot rather I gave her a shiner than holler cop, especially considering she had a little difficulty with the police down in Miami last winter."

"Then why didn't you just take the cuff links back, and let it go at that?"

"And have it get around that I'm a sucker? Never."

Ellen stared at him helplessly. It was obvious that he felt slapping Delphine was not only a justified response, but, given the circumstances, downright lenient treatment. And despite her flare of vengefulness, possibly Delphine thought so to.

She said, "I guess I just don't understand."

His face softened. "No, you don't. That's what I like about you, that you'd never be able to understand."

The silence lengthened. Then, to her relief, she heard the houseman say, "So you're back, Mr. Vandering," and knew that in a few minutes the visit would be over.

sixteen

Around six in the evening two days later, after a long sail in the rented catboat, Len drove Ellen and Cecily home. As she got out of the car at the foot of the porch steps, Ellen's face and body felt that pleasant glow produced by several hours' exposure to sun and salt spray.

Smiling, Len looked past Ellen to watch Cecily run up the steps. "Funny thing. That child never used to run. But I didn't realize it until recently, when she started to." He paused. "How about driving to Montauk for dinner tomorrow night?"

"That sounds wonderful."

"Pick you up at seven, then."

Hearing his car pull away, she went up the steps. As she entered the hall, Martha emerged from the living room. "Western Union phoned about an hour ago. They had a telegram for you."

"What was the message?"

"I wrote it down." She nodded toward the telephone table at the foot of the stairs. "It's over there."

Moving to the table, Ellen picked up a slip of paper torn from the pad beside the phone. In a large, angular hand

165

Martha had written: "Arriving Kennedy Airport 9:20 P.M. via American Airlines. Love, Mother and Dad."

Ellen stared at the message in bewilderment. One night less than a week before she had talked to her parents over long distance. They had said nothing about a trip east.

She turned to Martha, who had lingered in the living room doorway. "Are you sure this is for me?" After all, almost anyone might receive a wire signed Mother and Dad.

Martha shrugged. "They said it was addressed to Miss Ellen Stacey, care of Mrs. Janet Vandering. I guess they put her name on it so Western Union would know where to phone."

Yes, Ellen thought, but why hadn't her parents telephoned her several days ago about their plans? Even if they had decided upon the spur of the moment to come east—which would have been most unlike her commonsensical parents—they could have telephoned her before they began the long drive from Santa Monica to the Los Angeles airport.

Then fear clutched her. Perhaps they had news for her—news so distressing that they wanted to be with her to comfort her when she received it. If either of them had received some adverse verdict from a doctor . . .

Turning, she began to climb the stairs. Martha called, "If you're going to drive to New York, you'd better have something to eat first."

"No time," Ellen called over her shoulder. "I'll have something at the airport."

Since most of the rush-hour traffic had vanished from the freeways, she was able to reach Kennedy before nine o'clock. She left the station wagon in the parking lot oppo-

166

site the American Airlines Building and, trying not to think of the time eight years before when she and Richard and Beth had entered this huge waiting room, made her way through the crowd to the information desk. The nine-twenty flight, she was told, would be on time. Going into the coffee shop, she ordered coffee and a tuna sandwich. But when the sandwich was placed before her, she found that her throat was too dry to swallow. She sat there, sipping coffee, and thought of those two beloved people—one perhaps with grief and a terrible foretaste of loneliness in the heart, the other with resignation—on that plane hurtling toward New York.

A voice on the loud-speaker announced that passengers on the nine-twenty flight from Los Angeles were being discharged at Gate Seven. Ellen hurried down a sloping corridor in time to see the first of the passengers—three uniformed Marines—emerge from the landing ramp into the building. After that they came in a flood—matrons dressed out-of-towner style in flowered prints and white shoes and white hats, travel-rumpled men, a girl in pink cotton shorts who had a baby in her arms and pink plastic rollers in her hair, more servicemen. But no tall man with a ruddy face and white hair, no slender woman with blond hair fading to gray. All around her people were greeting each other, shaking hands, embracing. Then, after no more than two minutes, the last of the passengers and those who had come to meet them had disappeared into the terminal's main waiting room. Except for a uniformed clerk, the railed-off enclosure beyond Gate Seven was empty.

She approached him. "Was that all the passengers on that flight?"

A brunette stewardess, emerging from the landing ramp, answered for him. "Yes, they've all left the plane."

"But my parents were supposed to be on it!"

The stewardess said, instantly sympathetic, "Let's go look, shall we?"

Ellen followed her down the ramp and onto the dimly lighted plane, with its litter of discarded newspapers and magazines, its air that smelled stale now that the ventilation system had been turned off. No one at all occupied the rows of seats in first class, or the much longer rows in economy. The stewardess looked into each of the lavatories, and reported them empty, too.

As she accompanied Ellen up the ramp, she said, "Perhaps your parents missed this flight and took the next one. Why don't you ask up at the arrivals desk when the next plane is due?"

"Yes, I'll do that," Ellen said, anxious and bewildered. "And thank you very much."

Halfway up the corridor to the main waiting room, a thought struck her. How could she be sure her parents had even left California? She herself hadn't received that wire. She had only Martha Barlow's word for it that Western Union had telephoned.

On the upper level, she stopped and looked in her change purse. Apparently she had almost two dollars in silver. At the cheap night rate, that would be more than enough to call California. If there was no answer, she'd wait until the next flight arrived. She went into a phone booth, dropped a dime in the slot, and then, at the operator's request, deposited more coins. Three thousand miles away a phone whose exact location she visualized—on the desk there in the den-TV room—rang four times. Then her mother's voice said,

"Hello."

"Hello, Mother. How are you?"

"Why, Ellen! Is anything wrong? You sound rather strange."

"No, I just got to thinking about you. How are you?" she asked again. "And how's Dad?"

"We're both just fine, dear. We spent two hours on the golf course this afternoon. Your poor dear father still thinks he can make a golfer out of me. And now we're about to have dinner out on the patio. It's only around seven out here, you know." She paused. "Are you sure you're all right?"

"Of course. Why?"

"Well, we talked on the phone only a week ago. And so I wondered—"

Better give some explanation. And better hang up before the operator, breaking in to ask for more money, betrayed that this was a pay phone, because then her mother would wonder about *that*.

"Oh, I had a silly dream last night, something about you and Dad planning a trip. And in the dream it seemed to me that one of you wasn't well."

"That was a silly dream! We're both healthy as horses. And you know how your father hates to travel."

"I know. Well, I'll write you a letter soon."

"You do that, dear. Stamps are cheaper than phone calls."

"Good-by, Mother."

Hanging up, she crossed to the building's exit, scarcely aware of the people streaming past her. Why should Martha have lied to her? True, she had no illusion that Martha liked her. Probably Martha didn't like anyone except her cats. But, after that brief flare-up that first day, their relations

169

had been reasonably amicable. Why should Martha have played such a trick, and a deliberately cruel one at that, since as she was leaving the house she had confided to Martha her fear that one of her parents might be seriously ill? Ellen could think of no reason.

Unless Martha or someone else—someone who had pretended to be calling for Western Union—had wanted to make sure that she was well away from the house tonight.

But that, too, was absurd. Why should anyone want to get her out of the house tonight?

Just the same, her steps were swift as she approached the parked station wagon, and her fingers, as she inserted the ignition key, were not steady.

In Cecily's dream, hail suddenly fell from a clear blue sky onto the catboat deck where, a moment ago, Ellen had been sitting. Then, as she came groggily awake, Cecily realized that June bugs must be bumping against the window screen of her darkened room. That was odd. Usually it was only when the light was on. . . .

The splattering sound came again. Not hail. Not June bugs. Pebbles, probably about the size of those out there in the circular drive.

Limbs already weighted with dread, she threw back the blanket and crossed the shag rug to the window. No moon tonight. Just starlight glimmering on the drive and on the ribbons of ground mist that hovered a few feet above the front lawn.

Then she saw him—a dark figure standing only a few feet beyond the front wall of the house, hidden by the porch from anyone who might glance out a window in the other wing. He must have seen the flutter of the white embroidered curtains as she parted them, because a flashlight shone for a split second, only long enough for her to see the thin face, illuminated from below, and the beckoning gesture of his raised hand.

For a moment she stood motionless, staring down at the lawn where a pale after-vision of that face floated. Then she backed away from the window. It was coming back, that feeling she had hoped never to have again, that shame, that sense of her own badness.

But something else was rising in her this time—an anger that blotted out the sense of shame. She wasn't bad; she wasn't! It was that man down there who was bad, and that other one, who must be down there somewhere, too. People that bad ought to be arrested.

Go out into the hall and call the police? No, no! Long before the police got there, those two would come into the house and kill her the way they killed Amy, and kill Cousin Martha, too, if she interfered, only probably Cousin Martha wouldn't even hear anything, because she took off her hearing aid at night and slept with her good ear in the pillow.

The anger was gone now and she had begun to be afraid —so afraid that sweat rolled down her sides under her nightgown. If only she could run out the back way to the garage and the Lindquists. But they'd be watching for that. She imagined them running out from the trees to grab her. . . .

Why was she just standing there? Get dressed, fast, and go outside to meet them. If she didn't, they would think she was calling the police, or trying to wake Cousin Martha, and they'd come in the house, and—

She crossed to the closet, groped for blue jeans and a sweater. Other clothing fell to the floor with a soft, slithering sound. She knelt, thrusting her hands beneath the fallen clothing until she found her sneakers. Ellen, she thought, as she pulled the blue jeans onto her legs. But no, better that Ellen wasn't here. If Ellen were, she would do some brave, useless thing like calling the police or trying to get to the garage.

The windowless hall was dark. Cecily groped her way, one hand trailing along a wall, to the landing, and then down the stairs, holding onto the rail. Her heart was thudding so hard that she almost felt the man waiting outside could hear it. She tried to quiet it by telling herself that there was nothing to be afraid of, not if she got out there fast. They wouldn't do anything to her. They would just give her the envelope, and warn her again not to tell anyone, and then go away.

The lower hall, too, was in complete darkness. She tried to move straight ahead, right hand stretched out to grasp the bolt on the door. But she must have veered a little to one side, because she ran into something hard. She heard the impact of wood against wood, and the crash of shattering china, and knew that she had knocked over one of the big oriental vases and its teakwood stand.

Panic gripped her. Would the man outside think she had done it on purpose, hoping Cousin Martha would wake up? Hurry! Get out there and tell him it had been an accident.

Her groping hand found the door and its bolt. She shoved the bolt back, turned the knob, and moved out onto the porch, leaving the door open behind her. But when she had descended the broad front steps and looked to the spot where he had been standing, he wasn't there. Not knowing what else to do, she crossed the driveway to the lawn and stood shivering in the starlight, her gaze anxiously searching the curved wall of the surrounding trees.

A flashlight blinked on and off, twice. They were waiting for her, there on the path that led down to the beach. Hearing the seething of her own blood in her ears, she moved toward them.

seventeen

It was eleven-forty by the dashboard clock when Ellen emerged from the Vandering private road onto the circular drive. Feeling a mixture of indignation and formless anxiety, she had driven fast all the way from Kennedy. East of Shinnecock Canal, wisps of ground mist eddying above the highway and lying milky in the hollows—the same sort of ribbony mist she now saw hovering above the lawn—had forced her to slacken speed, but even so she had continued to drive faster than was prudent. Not bothering to take the car around to the garage, she got out and climbed the steps.

Apparently the hall lights were on, sending a dim glow through the living room windows. Perhaps Martha was up, and hadn't yet locked the door for the night. Yes, the knob turned under her hand.

Inside the doorway she stopped short, staring at the overturned teakwood stand and the shattered fragments of the Chinese vase. Who had upset it? Some member of the household? If so, why hadn't the mess been cleaned up? She stood there for a moment, listening. No sound. And the house had a strange, empty feeling. . . .

Anxiety sharpening to fear, she ran up the stairs and

174

turned into the west wing hall. At Cecily's door she called the child's name, then flung the door open. Enough light filtered up from the hall below to show her the empty bed with its flung-back covers. She flipped the light switch. The room was empty, its closet door standing open. Several garments dislodged from their hangers lay on the closet floor. Swiftly she crossed to the adjoining bath. It, too, was empty.

Aware of her quickened pulse rate, she crossed the landing and knocked on Martha's door. No answer. Pushing the door open, she turned on the light. Here, too, an empty bed with flung-back covers. Ellen stared numbly at the disordered blankets. Why should both of them have gone to bed, and then, apparently, got up in the middle of the night and just disappeared?

Empty of all thought now except the need to get to the Lindquists, she hurried downstairs and along the lower hall to the rear door. It was locked. Releasing the catch, she pulled the door open and ran through the ribbons of mist to the garage. At the top of the outside staircase she pounded on the door. "Wake up! Please wake up!"

After what seemed a long time a light came on inside the apartment. Lindquist, a heavy blue bathrobe over his pajamas, his graying brown hair awry, opened the door. Despite the mingled annoyance and alarm in his face, his voice was calm. "What is it, Miss Stacey?"

"Do you know where Mrs. Barlow and Cecily are?"

"Why, aren't they in the house?"

"No! Didn't you hear anything? Did a car drive up and then drive away?"

"We heard nothing. Did you search the house?"

"No." She hadn't even thought of it. She had been in too

175

much of a hurry to get to the Lindquists. Besides, there had been that empty feeling in the house. But maybe it wasn't empty. Maybe an intruder had herded them into some room, or down into the basement. She pictured them down there on the cement floor, arms bound, mouths taped, helpless to answer when she called their names. Pray God it was only because their mouths were taped that they hadn't answered.

She said, "I'm going to call the police."

Mrs. Lindquist, knotting a blue flannel robe around her, spoke from a doorway. "I'll call the police. Thor, you'd better get dressed and help Miss Stacey search the house and grounds."

Ellen said, "I'll wait out here."

"Very well. I'll hurry," Lindquist said, and closed the door.

Ellen stood there on the little platform at the top of the stairs, shivering despite the night's warmth, and listening to Mrs. Lindquist's voice as she told the police how to reach the Vandering house. Another picture was forming in Ellen's mind. Martha and some faceless person or persons driving away in a car, with Cecily as an unwilling passenger. Martha, whose story of a telegram had sent Ellen racing to Kennedy Airport tonight. Martha, whose poverty, as well as her hatred of Janet Vandering, might tempt her into a kidnap plot. . . .

The door opened. Lindquist, in trousers and a dark shirt, handed her a flashlight. "I'd better search the house. You could look around the grounds."

At the foot of the stairs, Lindquist hurried off toward the rear entrance of the house. Ellen moved toward the front lawn, alternately calling Martha's name and Cecily's, play-

176

ing the flashlight's beam over grass that looked black in contrast to the patches of hovering mist, and over the trees that encircled the grounds. Walking past the west wing, she crossed the graveled drive. "Martha! Cecily!"

A whimpering moan, somewhere to the right. She cried, "Cecily?" Again that moan. This time she could tell where it came from. The path leading down to the water. With the sense that everything within her had tightened itself into a knot, she hurried toward the gap in the trees. The flashlight's beam, shooting ahead of her, found the black-slippered feet, the plump bare legs lying across the path, the twisted hems of a yellow cotton nightgown and matching robe.

Martha lay with the upper part of her body off the path, between two maple trunks. In contrast to the dark blood soaking the front of her yellow robe, her face was white —an ominous, drained-looking white. Turning toward the house, Ellen screamed, "Lindquist!" Then she knelt beside the woman and laid the flashlight on the ground.

"What happened?"

The colorless lips stirred in the flashlight's glow. "Crash —woke me."

To save the woman's ebbing strength, Ellen said swiftly, "I know. The Chinese vase."

"Cecily—not in room."

"So you came downstairs, and saw the vase."

The whispering voice said, "Front door open."

"You came out to look for Cecily. You heard something, saw something?"

"Light."

"A light down here," Ellen said, aware that Lindquist stood beside them now. "You came here. And then?"

"Cecily with—two men. One—had knife—"

177

Ellen crouched there, motionless, aware of a cold nausea in the pit of her stomach. Cecily and two men. So it must have been true, after all, that story she had later denied.

Looking up, Ellen saw that Mrs. Lindquist, fully dressed, had joined them. In her hand was an acetylene lantern. Ellen said rapidly, "One of you please call an ambulance."

Lindquist nodded and strode away. Ellen turned her gaze back to the white face, the little gray eyes that looked glazed now.

"Did the men take Cecily away?"

"Don't—know. Heard car—drive off."

Picking up the flashlight, Ellen got to her feet. "Please stay with Mrs. Barlow." She turned and moved rapidly down the path onto the beach. "Cecily!"

A whimpering, indrawn breath.

Ellen swung the flashlight toward the left. Cheek resting against a tree trunk, the child sat huddled on the sand. Ellen ran to her, knelt, laid down the flashlight. As she grasped the thin shoulders, Cecily looked up at her. In the flashlight's refracted glow, the small face looked dazed.

"Cecily! Are you hurt?"

An almost imperceptible shake of the head.

"Those two men. Did they give you something?" In the distance, a siren wailed.

"Yes," Cecily whispered.

"Where is it?"

"I dumped it in the sand." The soft voice trembled. "I'm different now."

"Oh, darling!" Through her shock, her pity for Martha—poor, disagreeable, unfairly suspected Martha—Ellen felt a surge of gratification. "Of course you're different now. But it must have been in an envelope or something. Where is it?"

"Around here, I think."

Ellen picked up the flashlight. Its beam caught two empty little plastic packets—no, three—and a crumpled white paper envelope. There were scuff marks, too, revealing the sand's damp underlayer. Bringing the flashlight close, Ellen saw grains of white powder mingled with the dark sand. She could imagine Cecily, in terrified revulsion, grinding the dreadful white stuff into the sand with one sneaker-clad foot.

Gathering up the plastic envelopes and the paper one, she thrust them into the pocket of her light coat. The police would want to see them. "Come, darling." Reaching down, she helped the shivering child to stand. To judge from the sound of its siren, the police car had turned onto the private road.

Cecily's lips moved. "Those two men, did they—? Is Cousin Martha—?"

If the woman was dying, the child would have to know about it sooner or later. "We'll just have to wait and see, dear."

Cecily drew a sobbing breath. "I wanted to stay with her, or run to the Lindquists, but I was afraid they were—still around—"

"I know, dear; I know. Let's go up to the house now."

She led Cecily, not along the path where the woman lay, but through the trees sloping upward to the lawn.

eighteen

Ellen was awakened by a tap on her door and Mrs. Lind-quist's voice calling her name. She sat up in bed and stared groggily at the early-afternoon light streaming through the bedroom window. "Yes?"

"A detective to see you."

"All right. I'll be down in a few minutes." Feeling weighted with fatigue, she got out of bed and began to dress.

The hours between midnight and this morning's sunrise were a jumble of sounds and strange faces in her memory —police sirens, and the siren of the ambulance Martha Barlow had no need for by the time it arrived. Police moving over the grounds and through the house—East-hampton police, and later on police from Riverhead, the county seat. Plainclothes men asking questions of her, and of the Lindquists, and of Cecily. Looking small in a linen-covered armchair, hands folded in her lap, voice holding the hushed sound of shock, Cecily had answered. Yes, they had given her heroin before, three times before. She told about those times. No, she hadn't seen their car. She had just heard it start up on the private road. By that time she herself had run down to the beach. Yes, she could explain the light that had attracted Cousin Martha. One of the men, the short one, had dropped his package of cigarettes and had shone a flashlight around until he found it.

Summoned by Ellen's phone call, Howard Vandering had arrived shortly after two o'clock. Len Vandering also had been here for a while the night before, an expression of bewildered anxiety in his gray eyes as he looked from Ellen to the small, tense figure in the armchair. Who had called him, Ellen didn't know. One of the Lindquists, probably, or perhaps his brother had stopped to phone him on his way out from New York. Or perhaps some all-night radio station had carried a bulletin.

It was already dawn when Howard Vandering, looking dazed and broken, had put his daughter in his car and driven off toward New York. Soon after that the last of the detectives had left. Ellen had climbed through the cool morning light to her room and, well after sunup, fallen into exhausted unconsciousness. Now, descending the stairs, she felt lightheaded from lack of sleep.

A middle-aged man in a gray suit got to his feet as she entered the living room. "Miss Stacey? I'm Detective Monahan of the Riverhead police."

"Were you here last night?"

"No, I was off duty then."

"It's just that there were so many—"

"I know. You must be very tired of answering questions, so I'll make this brief." Reaching into his pocket, he brought out a sealed package of cigarettes and handed them to her. "Do you know anyone who smokes cigarettes of this sort?"

Wonderingly, she looked at the light green pack. It bore

181

a silver crescent, and words in graceful Arabic script. "I've never even seen a package like that."

"That's not surprising. They're of Lebanese manufacture, and have almost no market in the United States. The largest tobacco retailer in New York City stocks them—that's where this pack came from—but as far as we've been able to learn, no other dealer in this area does."

She said, handing the cigarettes back to him, "I don't understand."

"A single cigarette of this brand was found near the spot where Mrs. Barlow was murdered. Not a stub. An unlighted cigarette. Evidently it had been accidentally spilled from an opened pack."

Ellen nodded, remembering how Cecily had said that one of the men had shone a flashlight around, looking for the pack of cigarettes he had dropped, and thus inadvertently attracting Martha Barlow. Strange to think that if he hadn't dropped those cigarettes, Martha would still be alive.

"If so few of this brand are sold, couldn't that dealer in New York help you to find those men?"

"We're checking on that, of course. But probably the cigarette found down there on the path hadn't been bought anywhere in the United States. A lot of opium originates in Lebanon, you know. A man engaged in the drug traffic might have brought a supply of his favorite cigarettes from Lebanon into this country.

"Well," he concluded, "Thank you, Miss Stacey. We hope we won't have to bother you again today."

She had just closed the front door behind Dectective Monahan when the phone rang. It was Len calling. "I'd have phoned earlier, but I thought you'd be asleep."

182

"Yes," she said vaguely. "Have you heard anything about Cecily?"

"Howard phoned a few minutes ago. Cecily's with her mother now. Janet flew down from Cape Cod this morning."

"I'm glad." She paused. "Oh, Len! Who could have hired those terrible men?"

His voice sounded heavy. "I don't know. But it has to be someone who hates that child, or Janet, or Howard, or all three of them." After a moment he added, "I suppose you're too tired to see me now."

"Yes, Len, I am."

"And I guess you've forgotten about our dinner date."

She had. "I'm sorry, but I just want to rest."

"I understand. Well, I think I'll go to work. I may not get much done, but at least it will be a distraction. Good-by, Ellen. I'll phone you tomorrow."

At Mrs. Lindquist's urging, she ate a light brunch of orange juice, toast, and coffee, and then went back to her room. She exchanged her dress for a cotton robe and lay down. But, like an unwilling spectator at a jumbled, out-of-sequence film, she kept seeing people in her mind's eye. Dale Haylock, stumbling drunkenly along the beach, his face bitter and self-pitying in the bright moonlight. Amanda Mainwaring, eyes glassy-bright as she recounted her wrongs. Dan Reardon saying, across a luncheon table, "Sure. I'm a liar and a scoundrel. Just ask anyone." Len, removing the masks from the plaster faces of his "Family Group."

Around five in the afternoon she did manage to fall asleep, only to come rigidly awake half an hour later from a dream in which the whole exterior of the house had been bathed in a blood-red light, and she had run from one wing to the other in search of Cecily, and then had stopped, paralyzed and helpless, on the stair landing, her gaze riveted on a masked figure who climbed toward her, a hangman's rope coiled over his arm.

She lay there, heart still thudding from the terror of that dream, and her body soaked in perspiration. A swim, she thought. That might help.

It did, as long as the warm, silky water was soothing her body. But when she emerged onto the sand, her gaze flew to the spot where she had found Cecily huddled the night before. Dan Reardon, she realized now, had stood on almost that same spot the moonlit night when he had said, "You're beautiful."

Avoiding the path where Martha had lain, Ellen moved through the maze of trees toward the house. Here under the interlaced branches it was already twilight. She emerged onto the grass, her long shadow moving ahead of her. In another hour or so, it would begin to get dark.

Suddenly she wished she had gone into New York with Cecily and her father, or taken the train in today. But that, she knew, was foolish. If any danger threatened her, outside of that conjured up by her strained nerves, she would be far safer here than alone in her New York apartment. The Lindquists planned to sleep in the house tonight, and Thor Lindquist had a gun, a thirty-eight caliber revolver that Mrs. Vandering had bought for him the first summer she and Cecily had spent out here after the divorce.

Yes, she would be safe enough. But she hated the thought of lying awake in that house, remembering the story Cecily had told the police in that hushed voice, and imagining the child's helpless terror as she moved through the misty dark toward those two waiting on the path.

She had started up the porch steps when an idea came to her. She would call Len and tell him she had changed her mind about dinner. She would also ask him to spend the night in this house. They could stay up late, until she felt sure that she'd be able to sleep.

In the lower hall, still in her robe and bathing suit, she dialed Len's number. No answer, even though she let the phone ring eight times. Well, maybe he was taking a sunset walk along the beach.

She tried again after she dressed, and still again twenty minutes later. Still no answer. At seven-thirty she sat down to a dinner of broiled lamb chops and asparagus served by Mrs. Lindquist. As she had feared, it was strange and unnerving to sit alone at the table, aware of the empty chair at her right where Cecily always sat, and that even more tragically empty one at the other end of the table. In fact, she had wanted to suggest to the Lindquists that they all three have dinner at the big table in the kitchen, but fear of embarrassing them had restrained her.

When Mrs. Lindquist came in to remove the dinner plate, she also turned on the lamp. Soon it would be dark—completely dark. Should she, she wondered, call Dan Reardon? If he were out here, she had no doubt that he would be willing to sleep in this house tonight, or even drive her to New York. But for at least two weeks now she had had an ambivalent feeling toward him. On the one hand, she still felt flattered, even stirred, by the thought of his obvious attraction to her. But at the same time she found it disturbing that he lived part of his life in a world she couldn't understand—a world where Delphines stole cuff links, and where men blacked their eyes, less out of rage than out of determination not to appear a "sucker."

If only she could get Len on the phone.

Suddenly she realized the probable explanation of why she hadn't been able to. He had planned to work, he said. Sometimes, perhaps always, when he worked, he muffled his phone. The last time she and Cecily were at his little beach house, she had watched through the door of the bedroom as he turned the phone's sound control to soft, put a pillow on top of the instrument, and a blanket on top of the pillow. Before he moved to his easel, he had closed the bedroom door behind him.

True, he had probably stopped work by now. But it could well be that he had forgotten to unmuffle his phone.

Mrs. Lindquist came back into the room, carrying a tray which held lemon ice and a small coffee cup. Ellen said, as the housekeeper set dessert before her, "I think I'll drive to Mr. Vandering's beach house. I have something to talk over with him."

Mrs. Lindquist straightened. "Maybe you'll think it's none of my business, but I think you ought to go to bed. You look tired."

"I'll be all right. It isn't far to his place."

"The left front tire on the station wagon is pretty worn, Miss Stacey. My husband has ordered new tires, but when he phoned the shop today, the man told him they weren't in yet."

"Then I'll drive slowly." Why was Mrs. Lindquist so insistent about her remaining in the house?

"After last night," the housekeeper said, "I wouldn't think you'd want to go driving around in the dark. I'd think you'd want to stay here, where you'll be nice and safe."

Nice and safe. Somehow the phrase awoke in Ellen the opposite feeling to what the woman must have intended.

Ellen said, rather sharply, "No, Mrs. Lindquist. I'm driving over there."

When the station wagon emerged from the private road onto the highway, Ellen looked to her left and saw a first quarter moon hanging low in the west. By the time she had driven through the village of Amagansett, though, and turned off onto a road leading to the fishhook-shaped point of land where Len's cottage stood, the moon had set, and she moved beneath a black sky spangled with stars.

She was out on the point of land now, driving past modest summer cottages. A week from now, after the city schools had closed, most of these houses would be occupied by women and children, waiting for the head of the house to join them on Friday night. But now, apparently, only one was occupied. The rest stood dark and shuttered.

The point of land had begun to curve. Looking across the quiet, star-glinting water of the bay, she could see Len's cottage set high on its stilts, the last house on the point. Light shone from its broad front window onto the sundeck. Thank heaven he was home.

She drove onto the packed sand where the Austin-Healey stood, parked beside it, and turned off her engine. She became aware of sounds she had come to associate with Len's house—the gentle lap of the incoming tide against a small pier, the splash of a fish breaking the black water and then falling back, the disturbed twittering of the barn swallows which, Len had told her, nested each year beneath the loftily perched cottage.

When she reached the foot of the outside stairs, the light on the sundeck above her came on. Len must have heard her car. She found him waiting in the open doorway. "Ellen! Come in."

187

Stepping across the threshold, she took a quick glance at the small dining table, where the remains of his dinner rested on a plate. She said, with a rather shaky smile, "You didn't answer your phone."

He looked blank. "My phone? But it hasn't—" Then: "Oh, Lord. I forgot to unmuffle it. Sit down. I'll be with you in a minute."

As he moved toward the bedroom, she sat down in a chair of molded white plastic and looked at the remnants of his meal. The bone from a small T-bone steak. Crumbs of what had probably been onion rings. The core of an artichoke. Why was it that men always cooked well for themselves? No tuna sandwiches eaten by the kitchen sink for them.

Looking through the bedroom doorway, she saw him toss a pillow back onto the bed and then turn the phone upside-down to adjust the sound control. "There," he said, coming back into the room, "I'm once more in touch with the outside world. Now what's wrong, Ellen? Not that I'm not glad you came, whatever your reason."

"There's nothing wrong, not really."

"Which means that there is."

"No, I just felt nervous."

"And who'd have a better right. Fortunately I have lots of cures for nerves. Vodka, gin—"

"No, thanks. But could I have some coffee?"

"I was just going to make some. Now sit still." He went into the tiny kitchen.

She didn't sit still. Restlessly, she wandered over to the easel and looked at the canvas propped upon it. He had been painting the scene from his own front window—the bay, a small wooded island, a sailboat heeling in the breeze.

188

"I like the new picture," she called.

He called back, over the sound of running water, "It isn't finished yet."

She started to turn back to her chair, and then stood transfixed, staring with numb incredulity at something on his littered worktable. No, there could be no mistake. There it was among the oil paints in tubes, paint-stained rags, and brushes thrust in old glass jars. A rumpled cigarette pack, perhaps empty, perhaps with a few of its cigarettes remaining. A light green pack, partially hidden by a paint-stained cloth, but most of its silver crescent and part of the flowing Arabic script clearly visible.

"So it's Len," she thought. In that first moment she felt no emotion, but only a sense of profound shock.

They had been here in this room, those two unspeakable men, or at least one of them. When? Last night, before they went to Janet Vandering's house, and forced heroin on her little girl, and stabbed Martha Barlow to death? Or had they been here today, to receive their payoff, and perhaps a tongue-lashing from Len about that unscheduled murder? Anyway, one of them had left that cigarette pack. And Len, turning back to his work—or had he begun it yet?—with that strange, utter absorption of his, hadn't noticed the pack. And even if he had, he would have seen no reason to destroy it. How could he know that one of his hirelings had dropped a cigarette of that brand back there on the path?

With actual physical nausea, she recalled that she had thought that she could fall in love with him, if she would let herself.

"Ellen!" Staring in sick fascination at that crumpled pack, she hadn't been aware of his approach. He said, close beside

189

her, "What is it? What are you staring at?"

She swung around to him, stretching her lips into a rigid smile. "Nothing. It's just that I felt—I might faint."

He grasped her upper arms. "You'd better lie down."

She forced herself to endure his touch. "No, I'll be all right. But I think I'd better go home."

"That's foolish. If you feel faint, you shouldn't drive."

"I feel better now." Again she smiled that rigid smile. "Please, Len."

His gaze searched her face. She hadn't fooled him, not entirely. The gray eyes held puzzled suspicion.

After a moment his hands released her. "All right. But I'll follow you in my car to see how you're making out. Wait until I get my car keys."

Did he suspect she knew something, even though he couldn't guess how she knew? If so, he would be thinking about that as he followed her toward the Vandering house. She pictured the Austin Healey suddenly accelerating, forcing her own car off a dark, deserted road. . . .

He had disappeared inside the bedroom now. She whirled, opened the front door as swiftly and silently as possible, and ran down the steps.

nineteen

She was inside the station wagon, fingers shaking as she turned the key she had left in the ignition, when she heard his shout. The sound seemed to come from the sundeck. A moment later, just as the engine roared into life, he appeared at the corner of the house. As she backed, he stood in the glare of her headlights for perhaps two seconds, and then, whirling around, lunged toward the foot of the stairs.

Thank God, she thought, backing onto the road. He must have raced after her without first picking up his car keys, and now he had to return for them. That gave her a longer lead. With luck, she could reach the Easthampton police before his Austin Healey caught up with the slower station wagon. As she drove, feeding the engine as much gas as she dared to on that narrow road, she kept looking into the rear-view mirror. He wasn't following—not yet.

The road had begun to curve. Just ahead was the cottage with the lighted window. Stop there, phone the police? No, she decided swiftly. On a week night, chances were excellent that the man of the house was in the city. She would probably find a lone woman there. If he came in, while she was still dialing the police . . .

The road had curved sufficiently now to afford her a view over the water to Len's house. At the foot of its staircase, something red gleaming in the light pouring down from the sundeck. The Austin Healey. Why hadn't he started after her yet?

Then, with a tightening of her stomach, she realized the probable reason. He must have stopped beside the littered table, his gaze searching it. By now, perhaps, he had seen the one alien object there—that cigarette pack—and realized that somehow it had given him away. She imagined him striding into the bedroom to take a gun from a closet shelf or bureau drawer, then hurrying toward the staircase.

Five small cottages, standing close together, cut off her view momentarily. When she again looked across the water, her heart gave a painful leap. The red car was backing out of the light that still streamed down the staircase. Her foot pressed harder on the accelerator.

She was off the point now, moving along a road solidly walled by trees. The headlights of an approaching car struck through the windshield, and for a moment she thought of braking to stop, getting out into the road, and waving her arms for help. But no. By the time she had made herself understood, the Austin Healey would have caught up with her. Seconds later she was glad of her decision. As the station wagon and an old black sedan passed each other, she caught a glimpse of a white-haired woman hunched over the wheel in grim concentration.

A series of curves ahead. Reluctantly slowing speed, she went around one curve, then another. Still no pursuing headlights in the rear-view mirror. But on this winding road he could be only fifty yards or so behind her without her knowing it.

An explosive sound. For one terrible split second, she thought it had been a gunshot. Then, feeling the car swerve, hearing the flop-flop of limp rubber over asphalt, she knew that Mrs. Lindquist had been right about that weak tire. She fought the wheel, remembering not to put on the brakes or slacken speed too abruptly. After a few seconds that left her weak and perspiring, she brought the car under control. As it jolted forward over the road, she thought despairingly, "What now?" Abandon the car, try to hide among the trees?

Then, with a wave of relief, she remembered that there had been a lighted filling station along about here, perhaps just around the next curve. She drove on, aware of a grinding noise that told her the steel rim was cutting through the flaccid tire.

Turning the curve, she felt sick with disappointment. The station was there, all right, but closed for the night. The only light, a green-shaded one affixed to the wall above the station house door, shone down on a sign that said "Frank and Harry's Super-Service." But at least there was a phone booth, standing to the right of the gas pumps but closer to the road. She could hide the car and phone.

The car jolted over gravel as she drove it behind the garage. She got out, closing the door quietly, and ran to the phone booth. She was inside it, and just about to close the door, when she heard a car approaching at high speed. Shaken by the thought of how close she had come to closing the door, and thus automatically switching on the overhead light, she took her fingers from the door handle and flattened herself against the booth's rear wall. Thank God, she thought, that she had worn a navy blue dress, rather than the pale yellow one she had almost chosen.

The Austin Healey shot past. The lamp above the garage

door shone far enough into the road so that she caught a glimpse of Len Vandering at the wheel, his face tight-jawed, set.

Quick, now. She closed the door, triggering the overhead light, and looked at the police's number, listed along with that of the fire department, on a card affixed to the phone. Then she looked in her change purse. A quarter, a nickel, and several pennies. Only the quarter would be of any use to her.

She was about to deposit the coin in the slot when she paused. Would the police pick him up right away? She could think of two good reasons why they might not. First, she would have trouble convincing the police of this fashionable summer colony that any member of the Vandering family should be arrested. Second, even if she did manage to convince them, their small forces might be otherwise engaged. And in the meantime Len, having failed to overtake her, would realize that he must have passed her, and would come driving back, more slowly this time.

Dan Reardon, she thought, weak with relief. His house was less than three miles away. He could call the police—they would listen to Howard Vandering's business partner—and then he would come to get her. Hands clumsy in their haste, she opened the phone book that dangled from a chain, looked up his number, dialed. What if neither he nor his houseman were there? For all she knew, Dan might be in New York, or Washington, or down in Florida.

But he wasn't. He himself answered the phone. "Ellen!" He sounded worried. "I tried to phone you about twenty minutes ago, but that housekeeper said you were out. Where are you?"

"Please, Dan. Please come and get me. I'm at a service

194

station called Frank and Harry's. It's on the road between—"

"I know where it is." From the tone of his voice, she
knew that she had communicated her anxiety to him.
"What's wrong?"

"Please just listen. Before you come for me, call the
police. Have them pick up Len Vandering. He's on the road
somewhere between here and Easthampton."

"Len Vandering! But my God, Ellen. Why?"

"Maybe you don't know it, but Martha Barlow was
stabbed to death last night."

"I didn't know it until about half an hour ago, when
Howard phoned from New York. That was why I was calling you. I wanted to find out how you were."

"Please, Dan! Listen. Len hired the men who killed her.
Don't ask me how I know. I just know."

After a moment he said in a stunned voice, "Are you
sure?"

"Yes! And he may kill me if he gets the chance. He just
drove by here, looking for me." Her voice rose. "And I'm
stuck here! The station's closed, and one of my tires blew
out. If he comes back—"

"Ellen! Listen to me. If you can move your car, hide it."

"I have; behind the garage."

"And *you* stay hidden. There are trees behind that station,
as I remember. To save time, I'll send Emilio for you while
I phone the police." He hung up.

Leaving the booth, she ran across the gravel to the
wooded, upward-sloping ground behind the garage. When
she had climbed about a dozen feet, she sat down on the
damp ground and wrapped her arms around her updrawn
knees. From here, looking down between the tree trunks,

she could see the darkened garage and the road beyond.

For the first time since she had seen that crumpled cigarette pack, she felt safe enough to turn her thoughts to Len Vandering's motives. Why had he tried to condemn his young niece to slow death? To get revenge on the brother he still hated, even though he denied it? To get his hands on the millions which, if Cecily died, would come to him? Or did his warped mind hold still another reason—something she couldn't even guess at?

Beneath her fear and revulsion, she felt a stir of pain. Despite the warning she had given herself—about his strangeness, about the unlikelihood that he would ever consider marrying her—she had been more than a little in love with him.

A light farm truck drove by, going toward Easthampton. A minute or so later an old jalopy rattled past from the other direction. For perhaps five minutes after that, there was no traffic. Then, with a surge of thanksgiving, she saw the black Bentley turn off the road, drive past the station house, and stop beside her own car. When the driver got out and called "Miss Stacey?" his accented voice pitched cautiously low, she was already moving down the slope.

twenty

Once inside the car's luxurious rear compartment, she leaned her head back against the beige velvet upholstery. Her eyes, half closed, stared unseeingly through the glass partition at Emilio's head and shoulders. Still searching for the key to Leonard Vandering's behavior, she went back to the beginning—that cold afternoon in May at the Cloisters.

As she stepped from the dim building onto the sun-flooded terrace, she had collided with a short, broad-shouldered man. At the time she had thought nothing of the incident. But now she realized that probably he had been the man who, at noon that day, had invaded the Mainwaring School, telephone repairman's kit in hand. Undoubtedly he had expected Cecily to leave the drug-filled envelope in her locker until the end of the school day, and then take it home with her. Instead she had placed the envelope in her purse and walked out of the school. He must have felt surprised and apprehensive. Apprehensive that in spite of her obvious fear, in spite of her silence up until then, she might take that envelope to her mother or to the police.

Ellen imagined him moving behind Cecily along the street, watching her board that bus, and then—in his own car, or by taxi—following the bus to the Cloisters. Watching from somewhere in the shadowy building, he must have seen the drugged child emerge from the restroom. Had he followed her out onto the terrace immediately, or waited awhile? Ellen couldn't know. All she could be reasonably sure of was that, hearing her footsteps, he had turned hastily back into the building, so hastily that they had collided in the doorway.

He must have been watching from somewhere nearby as she phoned Janet Vandering, and then drove off in a taxi with the child. At that point, surely, he had reported to Len Vandering. She could imagine Len saying, "All right, don't panic. I'll find out about her and decide what to do."

Finding out had been easy. The information she had given to Janet Vandering that first afternoon must soon have reached Len through his brother. The next afternoon, Len had sat in on her conversation with Howard Vandering. And that night, in Len's incongruously luxurious East Village apartment, she had indicated to him that in spite of that anonymous phone call—made by Len himself, or by one of his employees?—and in spite of Len's advice, she might try to befriend the child, just as Amy Thornhill had done.

Evidently that had been enough to turn the scales against her, because the next night, in that musty old theater on upper Broadway . . .

Lights approaching slowly along the road—a sports car's low-slung headlights. Swiftly, heart pounding, she flung herself sideways on the seat. The glow of headlights filled the Bentley's rear compartment, and then withdrew. She waited several seconds and then, sitting up, reached for the speaking tube. "Was that Mr. Vandering's car?"

198

"Yes, Miss Stacey."

Less than a minute later, the Bentley turned onto Dan Reardon's private road. Ellen closed her eyes, her tired mind still fumbling with questions. Why hadn't Len or those two men made further attempts upon her life? Certainly he had had opportunities as they drove around the countryside at night. Perhaps he had decided that, after all, she presented no threat to him. True, he must have had a bad moment when she referred to Cecily's account of the two men. But he couldn't have been too worried by it, not after she had made it clear that she would have disbelieved the story, even without Cecily's disclaimer of it.

The Bentley was moving down an incline now. She opened her eyes. Just ahead was the long white house and the attached garage, its wide doors raised. Leaving the car on the asphalt apron, she and Emilio walked toward the front of the house. Ellen could see the graceful yacht anchored near the long pier and, closer inshore, the small power boat.

Light filtered through the beige mesh curtains that screened the glass façade. Emilio rang the bell, and immediately the door opened. Dan said, worried dark blue eyes scanning her face, "So you got here."

She stepped over the sill. "We passed Len Vandering only a few minutes ago. You'd better call the police again and tell them."

He looked past her shoulder. "Will you take care of that, Emilio? Use the garage phone. Tell them just where you saw him, and how fast he was traveling."

"Yes, Mr. Reardon." Reaching into the room, the houseman closed the door.

Knees suddenly weak, Ellen sank into a high-backed

199

wooden armchair of Spanish design. Facing her was the partially closed door of the den. Fleetingly she thought of the day when, after Len Vandering had left them in that room, Dan had explained to her why he had blacked Delphine's eye. Strange to look back on that afternoon and realize that then it was Dan whom she had considered brutal and more than a shade corrupt.

Seated opposite her on another high-backed chair, Dan said, "All right, Ellen. What happened?"

"A detective came to see me this afternoon. He handed me a package of cigarettes—"

She told of the detective's questions, of her decision to drive over to Len's cottage, of the crumpled green pack she had seen on his littered worktable. As Dan listened, the astonishment in his face gave way to a grim and growing anger.

At last he said, "Does Vandering know about the cigarette found near the body?"

"Not from me. Not from anyone, I imagine, or he wouldn't have left that pack on his worktable."

"Yes, that figures. Did you say anything at all to him about it?"

"No. I panicked at the thought of him following me on those dark roads, so I just ran."

He looked at her for a long moment. Then he turned his head toward the partially open door of the den. "All right," he said in a voice colder and harder than she had ever heard him use, "come on out."

Perhaps two seconds passed. Then a stocky man, followed by a tall one with a long, thin-lipped face, stepped from the darkened den into the living room. Stopping just a foot or so beyond the doorway, they stood there with almost iden-

200

tical expressions of sullen apprehension. Ellen stared at them, knowing even in that first instant who they were, and yet too numb with surprise to feel anything at all.

"You stupid bastards," Dan said quietly. "You blundering—"

While Ellen listened with dazed incomprehension, he cursed them for at least a minute in an even, almost monotonous voice. Then he broke off to say, in a tone that was merely pettish, "Why the hell do you have to smoke, anyway? Why does anyone?"

The shorter man said defensively, "I didn't smoke while we were waiting for the kid. I know better than to take a chance of leaving butts around."

"I should hope so." Again Dan's voice was cold and hard. "You were recommended as being exactly what I needed—experienced men with no police records, and therefore, presumably, a few brains. But now I realize you've just been lucky so far."

The stocky man shot him a sullen look. "It was hot there under the trees. I took off my coat, and I heard something fall, and I looked around with the flashlight until I found my pack of cigs. I'd have looked around better, except that this fat broad showed up—"

"Because of the damn flashlight! You didn't tell me it was your own fault you had to kill her. You let me think she just happened to head for the right spot."

In the brief silence, Ellen's stunned mind struggled to comprehend. It wasn't Len Vandering to whom the heavy-shouldered man must have reported after she and Cecily had driven away from the Cloisters that cold May afternoon. It wasn't Len who gave orders to these corrupters of Cecily Vandering, these murderers of Martha Barlow. In-

201

stead, it was the man seated only a few feet from her now. Deep inside her, a mortal terror was gathering. But on the surface she felt much as she had when, emerging from the subway one afternoon, she had walked two blocks south thinking that she moved north. In the seconds before she had been able to regain her sense of direction, she had felt what she felt now—a dizzying disorientation, a sense of the whole universe swinging around her as the poles reversed themselves.

Hands gripping the carved arms of her chair, she jerked her head around to look at the front door. The tall man must have seen her movement because, casually and yet swiftly, he crossed to the door and stood leaning against it. Without raising her eyes to his face, she turned her head away. She was in no danger, she told herself, trying to master that gathering fear. No matter how ruthless Dan had been with the others, he wouldn't hurt her or allow his men to. He was too fond of her.

Dan was saying, in that hard voice, "All right, Barney. One time or another you handed Vandering a pack of those stinking Lebanese cigarettes of yours. Or maybe just part of a pack. Now when was it?"

The answer came sullenly. "If he's a tall, blond guy, it was only a few days back. He walked out to the yacht while I was polishing the midship rail, and asked if I had a couple of spare cigarettes. Said he'd run out, and didn't know anywhere close to buy some."

"So you just handed over a pack." Dan's voice was heavy with disgust.

"Not a whole pack. Just what was left in the pack in my shirt pocket. After all, I still had plenty from my last trip. I guess he didn't like them, though, because I saw him toss

202

the one he'd lit into the water and then drive off." Heat came into his voice. "How was I to know what was going to happen? And how was I to know he wasn't okay? I saw him walk out the front door and straight out to the pier. I figured you'd have got on the telephone to the yacht if you'd wanted us to be careful, or go below decks, or something."

"I didn't see him go out there. I was in the study because of my damned sinuses. And Emilio was back in the kitchen."

Emilio. With a surge of short-lived relief, Ellen recalled that Emilio had gone to phone the police. . .

And then she realized that of course he hadn't. That order had been given solely for her benefit. For a weirdly detached moment, she wondered how Dan kept his houseman in line. An enormous salary? No, probably something in Emilio's past. Illegal entry into the United States, perhaps, with a capital charge hanging over him in some other country.

Dan had turned to the tall man. "Joe, why didn't you try to stop a bonehead play like that?"

"I didn't even see the guy walk out there. I was painting the stack, and I'd moved around to the stern side." He added, almost as defensive as his companion, "When you called us down here, you told us to keep busy on the yacht daytimes, so we'd look like regular crew."

"Well, it can't be helped now."

Even before Reardon turned toward her, Ellen somehow knew that he was going to. His expression as he faced her was a complicated one, coldly determined on the surface, and yet with regret underneath, and even something that resembled pain.

She blurted out, without knowing she was going to, "You told these men to try to kill me, didn't you?"

For a second those dark blue eyes seemed to flinch. Then he said, "Look, Ellen. Amy Thornhill might have caused us a lot of trouble, if we'd let her. So when I heard about you, someone else who showed signs of attaching herself to the kid, I got worried. That night I had Joe phone you a warning but it did no good. The next afternoon you turned up in Howard's office, asking about Cecily. And so it seemed wise to arrange an accident, if it could be done without too much risk.

"Besides, you were only a name to me then," he went on, as if that made it all right. "I didn't even meet you until the next day. And I tried to protect you from then on. I didn't get you out of the house last night just so you wouldn't interfere. If there was to be any rough stuff, I didn't want you to get hurt."

"But why?" she asked incoherently. "Why any of it? A little girl like that. Trying to make an addict of her—"

"You're wrong, Ellen. I'd have had to get the stuff to her more often if I'd wanted to make sure she was hooked. That would have been dangerous and unnecessary. All I needed to do was to distract Howard whenever he showed signs of getting his head together."

She cried involuntarily, "How you must hate him!"

"Hate Howard? I don't hate him. Does a blackjack dealer hate the sucker he's trimming?"

She stared at him, unable to make sense of his words.

He went on, his voice hardening, "Howard's been waiting to be trimmed since the day he was born. I knew that the moment I met him at the Midtown Club. I also knew he'd eventually ask me to help him out of his financial mess. Now when I tell him a company should go public, it does, and I buy up a controlling interest under street names. When I

204

tell him to sell another million in gilt-edged bonds and shove the money into some company, he does it. What's more, a couple of the companies he sold to me at a big loss—only he didn't know I was the buyer—weren't losing money, the way he thought. They were doing quite well."

He paused. "It's just a matter of bookkeeping, and of pushing Howard away off balance every once in a while. When he's in that state, a guy only half as bright as I am could steal him blind."

She said, unable to keep the loathing out of her voice, "And you've kept him off balance through his daughter."

"Sure. That kid is the only living person he cares about. And you always attack a guy at his weakest point."

No shame or regret in his eyes now. But then, why should she expect there to be? A man of the sort Len had warned her Reardon might be—only she hadn't listened!—a man who operated with one hand in the world of legitimate business and the other in the world of organized crime, a man who could turn to underworld connections to supply him with psychopaths like those two over there—why should such a man hesitate to destroy one child? After all, associates in the drug traffic who had supplied him with those two men profited from the destruction of thousands of children all over the world.

She cried, "Why didn't you kill Cecily? That would really have finished her father."

"Sure. He'd probably have shot himself, or at least folded up Vandering Enterprises and gone to Europe for the rest of his life. But that would have been like letting the sucker walk away from the blackjack table with most of his roll still on him. Howard still has the bulk of his money stashed away in government bonds. I mean to get it—every cent of it that I can."

She stared at his cold, calm face for a moment, and then burst out, "Why have you—"

"Why have I told you this? There's no reason not to. Even before you stepped into this house tonight, you knew enough to ruin me."

As she looked at him, not understanding, he went on, "You knew about that cigarette pack on Len Vandering's table. If you'd gone to the police about it, they'd have asked where the pack came from, and that would have led them to me. I'm sorry, Ellen, but I can't give you another chance to go to the police."

An icy coldness spread through her. "What—?"

Again that flicker of pain in his eyes. "I'm sorry," he said again. "We'll take the power boat to a point a few hundred yards off that beach of yours. If you're ever found, they'll figure you went for one of your nighttime swims. You just went out too far, that's all."

How had she ever been fatuous enough to think that he was too fond of her—too fond to take her life even though his own might be at stake? She whispered, "The police will know. They'll find my car, miles away—"

"Ellen, don't tell me I can't. The car will be found on the Vandering private road. I've got a supply of tires for all my cars in the garage. One is sure to fit that station wagon."

She said desperately, "Lindquist will notice the new tire."

"So what? He'll figure you had a blowout before you got to Vandering's place, and had a new tire put on while the garages were still open. And even if he mentioned it to the cops, they wouldn't bother to check it out, not in a case of accidental drowning. Anyway, they'd have a hell of a time tracing it. Garages out here in the boondocks don't record tire serial numbers."

Her thoughts scurried frantically, looking for a way out. But there was no way, not right now, with three men arrayed against her. No, four. Emilio was somewhere nearby, in the garage, or some other room of the house.

"Watch her," Dan said curtly, and got to his feet.

Her eyes followed him as he crossed the room, opened a door into a hallway, and disappeared. Looking at the other two men, she saw that the stocky one, seated now, was shaking a cigarette from a pale green pack. The taller one, still standing by the door, held a small gun in his hand, its muzzle pointed straight at her. As she stared at him, he smiled, revealing teeth that overlapped. The smile held neither mockery, nor nervousness, nor menace. It was the sort of meaningless smile with which he probably greeted acquaintances who meant nothing to him, one way or the other. And in its very lack of emotion, Ellen found it terrifying.

She looked down at the floor. No, no chance at all now. But later, when they were outside, in the dark . . .

From somewhere deep in the house, Dan Reardon called, "Bring her back here, Joe."

The tall man waved the gun toward the hallway. She got up and, on legs that felt made of wood, crossed the room. Aware that the gun was leveled on her back, she moved down a softly lighted hall paneled in redwood. "Next door to your left," Joe said.

As she crossed the threshold into a bedroom, she had an overwhelming impression of whiteness—white walls, white fur rugs, large white round bed. She thought, again with that grotesque sense of detachment, "Delphine must have loved this room." In the midst of all that whiteness, Dan Reardon stood with a gun in his hand. He said, "All right, Joe. Get out." Then, nodding toward a white chaise longue, "Put those on."

Numbly she moved toward the chaise. A man's maroon dressing gown lay on it, and the bottom half of a shallow, rectanglar box, holding something made of green and white flowered cotton. Dan said, "It's a bikini." He added, in a grotesquely reassuring tone, "I cut out the labels, but otherwise it's brand-new. I bought it for Delphine, and she never wore it." His voice hardened. "Go on, Ellen."

She moved to the box, took from it the cotton bikini, and then turned to look at him. For a moment she felt a surge of hope. In his eyes was a brooding look that must have been there that night when, from the shadow of the trees bordering the beach, he had said, "You're beautiful."

Then the look was gone. He said, "Open one of those wardrobe doors. You can undress behind it. Better keep your shoes on. Go on now."

He meant it. He didn't dare not mean it.

Carrying the bikini and the dressing gown, she moved to a tall white armoire decorated with gilt scrolls, and swung back one of its doors. Between the door and the wall, as she unbuttoned her navy linen dress and let it fall to the floor, she thought, "I wonder what he plans to do with my clothes? Burn them? Sink them in the bay?"

And with that thought a nightmare sense of unreality closed in around her. Recognizing its danger, she tried to fight it. They meant to kill her. They had to kill her. Unless she could shake off this will-numbing sense that nothing around her was real, unless she could plan some means of escape, this was the last hour of her life. Soon they would be forcing her head under the starlit surface of the bay, holding her there until the air rushed out of her tortured lungs and black water rushed in.

But that paralyzing sense of moving through a bad dream from which she would soon awake was still with her as, wearing the suit and the dressing gown and her sandals, she stepped out from behind the wardrobe door. With Dan following, she moved down the redwood-paneled hall. Its light seemed different now—the strange cold light that illuminates the landscape of a nightmare. In the living room, through that same light, the long face of Joe and the square face of Barney seemed to waver toward her and then recede. Dan's voice cut through a far-away, pounding noise which she vaguely recognized as the quickened beat of her own blood. "Emilio, bundle up her clothes with a weight and bring them out to the boat." Turning, she saw the house-man. His olive-skinned face, too, seemed to waver.

Then she was outside, moving between Joe and Barney as, each grasping an arm, they drew her across the beach. Not even the darkness or the drag of sand against her sandaled feet could break through that paralyzing numbness. But as she moved along the pier, aware of Dan's following footsteps, the sense of unreality lifted for a moment. She thought, "There'll be other boats on the water. If I scream . . ."

She had an impression of the small power boat there to her right, the white cube of its deckhouse slightly rocking. The men on either side of her brought her to a halt. A narrow band of something, a deeper dark against the darkness, flicked past her eyes. Then cloth of some sort, held taut by the man behind her, pressed painfully against her lips. Teeth clenched against the gag, she began to struggle, trying to wrench her arms free. Someone's hand, thumb and forefinger pressing into her cheeks forced her lower jaw down, and the gag slipped into place.

For a timeless interval, all the fight went out of her. She felt herself lifted in someone's arms, handed down to other arms, set on her feet on the gently rocking deck. Hands pulled her backward, forced her down onto the cushioned seat that curved along the boat's stern. Then one of them was sitting on either side of her, pinioning her body with their own, hands grasping her unresisting arms.

Footsteps along the pier. Something heavy struck the deck. The footsteps retreated. She looked at the dark bundle which lay halfway between her and the spot where someone —Dan?—yes, Dan—stood at the wheel. She thought of what was in the bundle. Some sort of heavy weight. And her linen dress, and pantyhose and bra, and her handbag. Now there would be nothing to indicate that she had been in Dan Reardon's house tonight.

Terror and rebellious rage surged through her. She tried to lunge free. Dan said sharply, "Don't bruise her!" Arms came across the upper half of her body, pressing her firmly against the seat back. She heard the engine catch. The boat, with no lights showing, moved away from the pier.

She stopped struggling. Better to save her energy. Better to wait until the boat stopped off that little beach. If she could escape them, even for an instant, perhaps she could dive overboard and, despite the gag parting her lips and teeth, swim underwater.

But she knew her chances were so small as to be almost nonexistent. She couldn't swim all the way to shore underwater. And when she came up—well, they didn't want to do it that way, but if they had to they would shoot at her, and keep shooting as long as was necessary. She thought,

210

"It's as if I'm already dead." Did prisoners, moving along a stone corridor toward a gas chamber, have this sense that they had already died back there in their cells?

They were well out into the bay now. Lights of a few fishing boats, some moving, some apparently at anchor, shone over the black water. But they held no hope for her, and perhaps wouldn't have even without that gag stretching her mouth. Dan, a dark figure at the wheel, kept the boat, its engine throttled to a low throb, well away from those bobbing lights.

She looked up at those other lights, spread across the dark sky. No help there, either. The stars glittered coldly, remotely, utterly indifferent to the fate of an obscure actress aboard a lightless boat, or that of a troubled child now temporarily safe in a New York City apartment, or that of a puzzled and anxious young man, driving the narrow dark roads in his futile search.

The throb of the engine ceased. The dark figure at the wheel turned, moved toward her, knelt. She felt his hands removing the sandals from her feet. A strange man, Dan Reardon. He had wanted her to keep her shoes on, lest the pebbly sand or the pier's rough planks hurt her feet. . . .

He stood up. "All right." His voice was flat, dull.

She knew then that her life was measured in seconds, and her apathy fell away and, in rage and desperation, she fought. She flailed out blindly as the dressing gown was stripped from her, clawed at the face of the man—Joe?—who lifted her in his arms, kicked and thrashed about as he lowered her, feet first, into black, chill water. Her hands, a moment before sinking fingernails into his arms, transferred themselves to the gunwale and hung on desperately.

Dan must have started the engine, because she heard a

low throbbing. Through it came his voice, harsh and urgent. "Finish it! Hurry!"

Hands thrust her head below the black surface. Salt water rushed into her partially open mouth. Other hands pried her desperately clinging fingers loose. She threshed free of the hands imprisoning her head, rose gasping to the surface. Something splashed into the water close beside her. The weighted bundle. Again two hands clasped her head at the temples, like a vise, thrust her under, and this time maintained their grip. She held her breath, trying to delay for another instant the moment when her bursting lungs would empty themselves to draw in black and salty death.

Confused sounds, up there in the world that in a second or two would no longer be hers. And light, seeping down to where she still struggled against the thrust of those hands and against the terrible need of her lungs.

The pressure of those hands lifted. She shot up through the water into dazzling light, into sounds of running feet and shouting voices and crackling gunfire. Gasping, she caught the gunwale and held on.

Figures, dark against the brilliant light, looking down at her. She wanted to cry out, but couldn't, "Don't! Just shoot me. I'd rather—"

Hands grasping her hands, drawing her upwards. She felt the scrape of the gunwale's edge down her legs. She stood swaying on the deck for an instant before an arm went around her waist and another under her knees, lifting her. Blinking in the glare, she gained a confused impression that it came from a searchlight on another, somewhat larger boat, so close alongside that the vessels bumped jarringly, parted, bumped again. The searchlight's glare bathed the strangers moving around her and Joe, standing motionless and with hands raised near the wheel, and the two dark figures sprawled on the deck near the stern.

"I don't think she needs it, but have you got a pulmotor aboard?" It was Len's voice, and it seemd to come from so far away that she felt surprised when, turning her head, she saw that it was he who held her in his arms.

If someone gave him an answer, she didn't hear it. Black mist had closed in around her.

Before she opened her eyes, she was aware of a gentle swaying, of mingled smells of salt water and diesel oil, and of something else—something that reminded her of rainy days. Opening her eyes, she found that she lay, covered by a man's coat of yellow oilskin, on a rough bunk. Down near her feet, Len Vandering sat perched on the bunk's edge.

He smiled at her. "How do you feel?"

"All right." The words hurt her raw throat. "Where—"

"You're aboard a boat operated by the Easthampton police, Marine Division."

She stared at another oilskin coat swaying from a hook on the cabin's rear bulkhead. "I'm alive," she thought. "I'm *alive*." She whispered through her raw throat, "Those men—?"

His smile vanished. "Two of them are dead. Another one's in custody. No, two. They're holding Reardon's houseman."

"Dan?"

"He's dead. They shot at us, but by the time we turned on the searchlight, we were so close that they didn't have a chance."

"Were you the—"

"The one who called the police? Yes. It didn't occur to

213

me at first. After you drove off like that, I went back to my worktable and looked at it. I couldn't see a damn thing that could have scared you, or even anything that hadn't been there the last time you were at my place, except that almost empty pack of lousy cigarettes I'd tossed there days ago and forgotten about."

But since the pack seemed to be the only thing that possibly could have upset her, he had thrust it into his pocket and gone out to search for her. He'd driven swiftly from his place to Easthampton and then, sure that he must have missed her, turned back. "I passed Reardon's Bentley with his driver at the wheel, but the passenger compartment looked empty."

"I'd—ducked down. I was scared of you."

"I don't wonder, now that I know what you must have thought when you saw those cigarettes."

Increasingly alarmed, he'd driven back to Easthampton and called the Lindquists, who told him Ellen hadn't returned. Finally, not knowing what else to do, he had gone to the Easthampton police, told them of Ellen's strange behavior, and showed them the crumpled cigarette pack.

The effect had been galvanic. The moment they learned where he had obtained the cigarettes, the police had dispatched two cars to Reardon's house, with Len riding in one of the cars to show the way.

"Halfway down Reardon's private road, we met Emilio driving out in the Bentley. When the police stopped him, they found several brand-new tires in the trunk."

One of them, Ellen realized, was to have been fitted to a wheel of her abandoned station wagon, but she felt too tired to talk about the station wagon just then.

Despite Emilio's protests that his employer was in New

York, they had put him in one of the police cars and driven down to the house.

"Both of Dan's other cars were there, but the power boat was gone, so one of the police went into the house and called the Marine Division to get the patrol boat ready."

At his request, they had allowed Len to go aboard the patrol boat. At first they had headed east, on the theory that Dan might be planning to move out of the bay into Block Island Sound and from there to the Connecticut shore. But an anchored fishing boat they had hailed reported that a power boat, traveling without lights and throttled to a low speed, had passed only a few minutes before, headed north. The police boat, its running lights extinguished, also turned north.

"Now and then we'd cut our engine to listen. The last time, we heard another engine up ahead. About half a minute later, it cut out. We moved up fast then and turned on the searchlight."

She whispered, "So much to tell you and the police—"

"I know, but just rest now. There'll be plenty of time later."

Plenty of time, she thought, with an overwhelming sense of thanksgiving, and closed her eyes.

twenty-one

Under a merciless August sun, Ellen and Len stared through bars at the zoo's buffalo, who, ignoring them, stared straight ahead. All around them were the sights and sounds and smells of New York City's most unattractive season. Perspiring men in mesh shirts through which dark chest hair sprouted. Heat-pale women leading children by their ice cream–sticky hands. Blaring transistor radios. Mingled smells of dust and hot asphalt and caged animals. But not for a moment did Ellen wish she was traveling a tree-shadowed Long Island road, or changing to a swimsuit in Janet Vandering's cool, lovely house. Perhaps someday she would be able to enjoy the Hamptons again. But right now she infinitely preferred the city and her three-room apartment.

The wonderful, the unbelievable part of it was that Len apparently preferred the city, too. When she had left the Hamptons the day after the police had finished their questioning of her, and driven to New York with the Lindquists, Len had remained in his beach house. But the next weekend, and nearly every weekend since, he had turned up in New York and called her for a date. And when he phoned her

216

last night, he had announced that he intended to occupy his East Village apartment "for a week or so."

Ellen said, "Cecily once confided to me that she thought of this buffalo as a captured black king someone had brought here."

"To me he looks like a bas-relief of an ancient Abyssinian. Were the ancient Abyssinians black?"

"I don't know." She went on looking at the buffalo and thinking of Cecily. What a pretty, pretty girl Cecily was going to be. Two weeks ago, just before Cecily and her mother had gone up to Cape Cod for the rest of the summer, she had celebrated her twelfth birthday in the Fifth Avenue apartment, with her father and Ellen and her Uncle Len among those present. She had worn a single pearl on a gold chain around her neck, and, for the first time, pale pink lipstick. Even though Ellen could tell that the presence of Cecily's father in the apartment was stirring old hopes, she also sensed that Cecily, no longer weighted by either terror or guilt, felt strong enough to move toward normal young womanhood even if those hopes were never realized.

Len asked, "Why are you smiling?"

"I was thinking of Cecily."

"Ellen, you ought to have children of your own."

"I'll take the idea under advisement. Unfortunately, in spite of Women's Lib—"

"Yes?"

"In spite of it, that's still something a woman can't accomplish by herself."

"I know. A collaborator is needed. And that's something I've had under advisement these past weeks, loath as I am to leave my loft and my fascinating neighbors for some damned child-oriented suburb. Of course, we wouldn't have to leave the East Village right away—"

He paused for a moment and then asked, "Would you care to go over to the Plaza and exchange views on the subject over something tall and cool?"

Ellen felt an ache in her throat, a pressure behind her eyes, and for a horrified moment thought she was going to cry. But after swallowing twice she managed to say, "Yes, let's do that."